New Beginnings

A GREENGROVE NOVEL

Acknowledgement

I would like to thank my family for the support and encouragement they have given me. To my wonderful daughters and husband, who didn't mind me asking odd questions. I would also like to acknowledge everyone at Softwood Self-Publishing, especially Maddy, who has supported me and helped me realise my dream. A special thank you goes to the staff at Cresswell Crags; after visiting for our wedding anniversary, going on a cave tour, I knew I needed to put it in a book.

Chapter 1

Jane

I stood in Lacy's back garden, worrying about my fiancé Peter, the warm summer breeze dancing across my bare arms. I watched as the sun set and remarked that it was so warm I didn't even need a cardigan. Peter and I had been engaged for just over six months, but instead of being the life and soul of the party that he used to be, he no longer wanted to go out, and whenever I did, whether it was on my own or with him, he would just moan about it. First, there was the Community Centre fundraising night and now this.

Tonight was a party to celebrate Lacy and my cousin, James, moving in together, and I found myself standing all alone with no fiancé by my side, because apparently, *he wasn't in the mood* to meet up with our friends and celebrate.

Despite that, I was determined to have a nice time. It hadn't been that long since Lacy and I had become friends, not that we were enemies before, but I had been stuck hanging around with Sarah. When we were younger, Sarah didn't like Lacy. That's putting it mildly, in fact; she made Lacy's life a misery, and even now I could see the affect it had had on Lacy and her self-confidence. But since

James and Lacy had got together, her confidence had begun improving.

Wearing a huge smile and a lovely flowery, flowy dress, Lacy came up to me and said, "I am so glad you came. It wouldn't be the same if you weren't here."

Just at that moment, James appeared. He put his arms around Lacy's shoulders and kissed her on the head. After checking to make sure she was alright, he turned his attention back to me.

After giving me a kiss on the cheek, he said, "Hi, cousin, where's Peter? Are you alright?"

The love between the couple was bouncing off them and, in all honesty, I will admit to being a little bit jealous.

"Yes, I'm fine. He said he wasn't feeling well. Congratulations on moving in together. I know I've said it before, but you both make an amazing couple."

Auntie May then came to join us. "Jane, darling, are you ok?" she asked while giving me the biggest hug you could imagine. I say 'aunt', but she's been more like a mum to me since my mum, her sister, died. Even before mum's death from cancer, when James and I were growing up, we used to separate our time between mum's and May's house. That allowed mum to work, which she needed to do after she divorced my dad, and, in some ways, it gave Auntie May the daughter she had always wanted. After my Mum and Dad got divorced, I never heard from him again. He didn't even come to mum's funeral.

"I'm fine," I lied.

"Now come on, Jane, I know you. You're not ok. Talk to me."

James and Lacy made a strategic retreat so May and I could talk.

"I guess it's seeing Lacy and James together. I'm not sure Peter and I share the love we're supposed to. Peter has changed. He doesn't want to go anywhere as a couple. When I try to talk to him about anything important, he just ignores me. Then he will go out with *his* friends. He's treating my house like a hotel. He won't talk to me, and honestly, it's making me miserable."

"You need to talk to him. But first you need to decide what you want. Do you still want to marry him?" Auntie May replied.

"Honestly, I don't know any more. But you're right, I need to speak to him. I need this sorted out one way or the other. I can't keep going on like this. I feel like I'm at breaking point, and each day I feel that I am losing myself and what I want out of life."

Auntie May gave me the hug that I had been crying out for and the reassurance that someone was there for me and that I wasn't alone.

"Thanks, Auntie. I'm going to go home and talk to him now. I'll find James and Lacy and let them know I am off."

With a new purpose, I gave my good wishes to the happy couple and arranged to meet up with Lacy on Wednesday evening. It didn't take long to get home. Unlocking the door, I was suddenly hit with Guns N' Roses blaring out of the stereo. Then I noticed the trail of clothes. They didn't belong to Peter, unless he had started wearing a short skirt. See-through blouse. Stockings. Following the trail of clothes to the bedroom, looking through the door that was ajar, I froze in horror. In my bed was my fiancé and Sarah, doing things that made me want to burn my mattress.

I could hear them. "Oh, Sarah, that's amazing, baby, yes, just like that. You are so much better than Jane. I'm slumming it with her. I need to get rid of her, and as soon as I find us a place to live, I will."

In shock and trying to hold onto my temper, I flung the door open wide.

"Sorry to bother you, but when you have quite finished, please get out and don't ever come back. The engagement is obviously off, so you'd better hurry up and find a place to live, because after tonight, you are no longer welcome here." With that, I threw the engagement ring at him, which rolled onto the floor with a *clang*. "When I come back in the morning, I don't want to see you here, and I never want to see either of you again."

I don't know how I did it, but after my little speech, I turned around before either of them could say anything, grabbed my handbag, and left the house. I refused to cry in front of them, but channelling my anger, I slammed the front door. As soon as I closed the door, I leaned against it and took a deep breath in the hopes that it would calm my shaking body. I could feel the anger zipping through my body. I was angry with myself because I had known things weren't right with our relationship and I should have ended it before now as it wasn't good for me. I was angry at Sarah who, until recently, was supposed to be my friend, but I guess in Sarah's world I chose Lacy over her, so this is payback. She looked like the cat that had got the cream. Lastly, I was furious with Peter. After ten years of being together, how could he do that to me. I knew things had been different with him recently, and in all honesty if he had decided he didn't want to be in a relationship with me anymore I would have accepted that, especially with the way things were lately. I would have called it off any day anyway if things hadn't changed. But to find him in bed with Sarah was just humiliating.

It was as if she was laughing at me because she knew what an idiot I had been to trust him, and I felt it. Although I was still shaking, I needed to get away from there and find somewhere to stay the night. I couldn't bear the thought of sleeping on that mattress ... Hopefully the pub would have a room. I didn't really want to drive into town to the hotel. First things first, I needed to ring James to see if he knew if there were any rooms left in the pub.

"Hey, Jane, are you ok?"

"Not really, no. Listen, I need a room for the night. Do you know if there are any at the pub free?"

"Why, what's wrong with your house?"

"I don't really want to talk about it, but when I walked in, Peter and Sarah were sharing a moment or two in my bed."

"Oh my God ... I-I'm so sorry. Come back to ours. Most people have left - its only mum and dad here now."

"I'm not sure if I will be great company, and I don't want to spoil your evening."

"Don't be silly. Oh, hang on, Lacy wants a word," James said as he handed the phone to Lacy.

"Jane, I don't know what's happened, but you'd better come here to your family, otherwise I will track you down."

I didn't even know how I had it in me to laugh at Lacy's words. "Ok, if you're sure."

"I am, and we will have the wine open for when you arrive." With that, she put the phone down, leaving me with no choice.

As soon as I got to their house, I realised that the party had indeed disbursed. It was lovely and quiet as I pushed the unlocked door. As soon as I entered, I was enveloped in a cuddle, which could only have come from Auntie May. I tried to speak, but my voice wavered and cracked, and the dam opened. Tears flooded down my cheeks.

I couldn't do anything to calm down the tears that I wouldn't let run free when I was leaving the house. I couldn't let Peter have the satisfaction of seeing me broken.

Auntie May led me to a sofa and sat me down next to Lacy. James had clearly told them what I'd said over the phone. Auntie May stroked my hair just like my mum did when I was younger while my head lay on her shoulder and Lacy holding my hand. I felt protected and cherished as my world crumbled. When I looked around the room, it was only the three of us there. James and Uncle Mike had retreated into another room.

"I don't mean to put anyone out. I just need somewhere to sleep tonight. I couldn't stay in the house after ... Hopefully when I go back tomorrow, he will have left."

"Don't be silly, my child. You are no trouble. Now, tonight you are coming home with me and Uncle Mike. Then tomorrow, when you are feeling up to it, Uncle Mike will take you home. But I want you to understand that there is no pressure. You can stay at ours for as long as you want."

"Thank you, Auntie."

"You don't need to thank me, and you know it. Now, I made you a cup of tea. Drink that and sit here with Lacy while I go and round the boys up and let them know where you are staying."

I did as I was told, but I didn't expect the tea to have a shot of whisky in it. I coughed and spluttered just as Auntie May left with a smile on her face.

Lacy smiled. "That woman is amazing. She knows exactly how to make you feel better. Although when I saw how much whisky she put in that tea … let's just say, I think you will be sleeping well tonight." She gave a soft laugh. "I want you to know, Jane, that if you need to talk to anyone, I will be here for you no matter the time, day, or night, and I know James feels the same."

"Thank you, Lacy, I really appreciate that."

Everyone came back in the room, and I was passed around for hugs before Auntie May and Uncle Mike decided

"I'll coming with you just in case he is still there and to see if he has left anything behind. I will be able to take his stuff to his parents' house. James has already rung this morning to check how you are and to offer his services if you need anything."

"Thank you, I would love you to come with me. I wasn't looking forward to going on my own, and I didn't want to put you both out any more than you already have been."

"Such rubbish, we aren't put out. In fact, we love having you to stay. If only it was in better circumstances. Now eat up you two. By the sounds of it, you have a busy day in front of you." my Aunt said before she placed a sausage sandwich in front of each of us.

We didn't go round to my house until after lunch. Instead, we spent the morning chatting and laughing about what my mum would say if she had been here, although it wouldn't be that different to what my Aunt May thought, only my mum would actually say it rather than keep it to herself.

After a relaxed lunch, true to his word, Uncle Mike came with me to my house. I went to unlock the door, but my hands were shaking. Uncle Mike took the keys out of my hands and entered the house, telling me that it was ok if I wanted to wait outside. The house was empty, just like I had asked. I gingerly went into the bedroom and looked at the wardrobe. Peter's stuff was missing. I was so relieved that I didn't need to deal with him that morning.

"Jane, I don't think Peter has left his key. Where would he put it if he had?" my uncle shouted to me.

"He normally puts it in the bowl by the front door."

"Oh right, it's not there. But don't worry, I will ring Stephan at the local DIY store and see if he has any locks in store. If he does, James can pick them up, then hopefully the house will be secure tonight."

I was so grateful that he had thought of that because I hadn't. Maybe it was because I was too busy thinking that what I needed most was a new bed. The thought of sleeping on that mattress just made me feel … dirty. I was glad I still had an old-fashioned wooden door rather than a new UPVC door that Peter wanted because it meant that the locks were easy to change, and my uncle should know how to do it as he had fitted the last one.

I found Uncle Mike in my living room and mumbled, "I need a new bed."

"Yes. Not to worry, we'll find one."

"Can I stay with you until it arrives?

"Of course, darling. We would love to have you stay with

us for as long as you need."

While we waited for James to bring the new lock, we sat on the sofa and discussed the next steps for the house.

I gazed about the house, memories of Peter staring at me like a sore thumb. The paint colour he had chosen in the bedroom. The furniture he had picked out. I felt sick.

"I need to redecorate," I stated.

"Happy to help with that. It will keep me out of mischief. Now, I think I hear James pulling up. Let's get these locks changed and take the bed outside for the council to come and collect it."

Leaving the father and son downstairs, I gathered together some clothes and essentials. It didn't take long for them to change the lock and put the old mattress outside. Gathering up my things to stay over, we then went back to Auntie May's for one of her weekly traditional barbeques.

In truth, I wasn't really in the mood for the barbeque. Living in a small village all my life, I knew that gossip would spread like wildfire, and I thought everyone would ask questions about what had happened with Peter, but I think that they had been threatened on the pain of death not to mention anything.

Once my destroyed love life inevitably became gossip, I

wondered who the village would think of as the villain? Peter or Sarah? Something was certain, though. With Auntie May on my side, it wouldn't be me. Just as I was thinking that, Auntie May approached me with a glass of wine.

"Here you go. Your uncle says that you want to stay with us for a couple of weeks, while you redecorate".

"Yes, is that ok? I don't want to be in the way."

"Of course it's ok. It will be a pleasure to have you. You know I miss you, and I can't think of a better house guest. Have you heard anything from Peter?"

"No, and honestly, I don't want to."

"I don't blame you. I worry about his parents, though. They're probably going to end up letting him live with them. If I see him, I will have a few words to say."

"Don't you think I am a little too old for you to fight my battles for me?" I said with nervous laughter.

"No. You will never be too old for that."

After a few glasses of wine, I still wasn't in the mood for any food, so as people started leaving and the tidying up was done, I went up to bed, and like the night before, as soon as my head hit the pillow, I was out like a light.

Chapter 2

Jane

Staying at my aunt and uncle's turned out to be one of the best decisions I had made. School hadn't started back yet, so other than a few meetings I had to attend. I was free to recover from the drama of the breakup. Although I wasn't sure that 'recovery' was the right word, but I couldn't think of anything close to describe what was happening. I have heard a few people's opinions as to what had happened between me and Peter, and although it shouldn't involve taking sides, it seemed to be that most people felt he was never good enough for me and I should have got rid of him long before now. There hadn't been pitying me, which I thought might happen. That would have been a nightmare. I really don't think I could have coped with that. The consensus was really on my side, which made it easier to handle. I lost count of the amount of people that had offered to help me move things out of my house. I had heard from Peter's parents, who also apologised for his behaviour and told me that they were sorry. I replied that they didn't need to be sorry. They had done nothing wrong and when I got the opportunity I would love to pop in and see them. I am not saying there are no sad moments, because there were, especially when I was on my own, lying in my old bedroom. I wondered what had happened. Where did I go wrong? Did I not notice what he was up to? I then got cross with myself because none of this was my fault. The blame lay firmly at Peter's door.

I spent the four weeks grieving the end of my relationship whilst having the hope of starting a new life. Lacy, my Aunt May, and I went out shopping to buy some new things for my house; things that I thought would look good in specific rooms. We had decided to redecorate the whole house. One of the things I realised during these shopping trips was that I had let Peter take over my opinions, and even though it was my house, it really was his tastes that had overtaken mine.

The first stroke of the paint brush, filled with buttercup yellow, on my light grey walls left me feeling free and in charge, as if I had risen up and almost returned to my old self again. James was putting wallpaper on the wall where my bed would be. The wallpaper I had chosen was a cobalt blue background with yellow buttercups and spring flowers decorated around it. The wallpaper matched the yellow I was painting with and didn't overpower the room at all; in fact, it made the room cosy and homely, which was just the look I was going for. It took us a week to complete the repaint of the bedroom and bathroom. I had written lists for every room as we slowly turned it back to my house, and with each room we transformed, I was slowly being transformed as well.

Next on the list was the living room. I had wanted a mantelpiece and electric fire put in, similar to the one mum used to have, but Peter didn't like it, so it never got done. I had been looking around when I was out shopping but I never found anything I liked. But the plan was that as soon as I did find something, my uncle and James would fit it for me. As soon as James had wallpapered the chimney breast with a lovely honey-coloured wallpaper with small gold flowers on it, Uncle Mike appeared with a mantlepiece and fire that looked exactly like the one my mum had when I grew up.

"Thank you so much" I cannot believe how much this looks like the one mum had, even down to the little bend in the grill there."

"That's because it *is* the same one. I rescued it years ago and I have kept it safe and maintained until you needed it. I am so glad that you need it now."

With tears pouring down my face, I couldn't speak. All I could do was cuddle him so tight he knew what I was trying to say.

"Jane, you forget I have known you a long time, and I knew in your heart that you didn't want to get rid of the fire. Now come on, dry your tears and help me put it into position while James drills the holes for us to give it pride of place where it belongs."

I cannot believe the amount of work James, Lacy, and my aunt and uncle put in to help my house look the way I wanted it to. I keep saying to them that I wasn't sure how I could ever repay them but the reply I got was: "You're worth it, and you never have to repay family."

It took four weeks to complete the full makeover of my house, and on my first night in my new home, I was sitting on the sofa on my own with a large glass of wine, exhausted after the long, busy day. I felt content and actually happy for the first time in weeks. Pleased with what we had achieved. The doorbell rang, and without even thinking about it, I opened the door. I cursed myself for my mistake. Standing on the other side of the door was a drunk Peter.

Just when I thought I had everything sorted, he had to make an appearance. Nobody had heard from him in the last four weeks.

"What do you want?" I snapped. "Go away."

"Oh, come on, darling, you don't mean that."

"Actually, I do. I think it's best if you just leave."

I tried to close the door, but he put his foot in the doorway to stop it from closing.

"Move your foot. I am not in the mood for you tonight, or any night to be honest."

"Oh, darling, I have missed you, and I know you have missed me too."

"What do you want?" I repeated.

"I want to know why you threw me out and ended our engagement."

My jaw actually dropped. How could he not know? He was drunk, I reasoned. "Move your foot and I will tell you."

As soon as he moved his foot, I slammed and locked the door in his face. The next thing I heard was him trying his keys in the lock. Thank heavens we had changed them. Having had no luck, he started banging on the door, shouting at me.

"You bitch! Let me in!"

My hands shaking, I rang the first number that came to mind.

"Hi Jane, what on earth is that banging noise?" James' voice felt reassuring.

"Peter is drunk. He's trying to get in." My voice shook as tears sprang to my eyes.

"Don't worry, I will be there shortly, but I will get his brother to come get him first. I think if I go anywhere near him at the moment, I might punch him."

With that promise, he hung up. I hoped they wouldn't take too long as I wasn't sure how much more either me or my door could take. My mobile buzzed in my palm. Lacy.

"James told me what is happening. While he gets hold of Stephen and comes round to yours, I thought it would help if I phoned you so you don't feel so alone."

I just cried down the phone, the tears running down my cheek.

"James has just flown out the door. Stephen is on his way, and James is going to meet him at yours. Under no circumstances are you to answer the door. James has the spare key, so you won't need to open the door to him, either."

"Thank you. I don't know what I would do without the pair of you or Auntie May and Uncle Mike. You have all been really good to me."

"I just hope the boys won't be too long. I'm surprised one of your neighbours hasn't called the police with all that noise going on."

"I think I've just heard two car doors slam. Hang on, I'm going up the stairs so I can check if it's them."

"Just be careful. By the sounds of it, Peter is imitating a raging bull, and if he sees you looking out the window, who knows what he will do? But I doubt it would help calm him down."

"I've never heard him like this. I'm just glad the locks were changed and he couldn't get in. He's never been violent before, but … I hardly know him anymore."

"It's probably because he has lost his meal ticket and now he has realised what an amazing person you are. It's gone quiet there. Do you know what's happening?"

"No. But I think James has just come in, so I'd better go downstairs."

"Goodnight, and don't worry if you need to come here tonight to sleep. There is a sofa with your name on it if you need it."

"I'll see what James has to say. Night."

Just as I put the phone down to Lacy, James called my name from downstairs. As I was descending the stairs James started to talk to me.

"Are you ok, Jane? Stephen has managed to get Peter in the car and is taking him back to their parents' house."

By the time I got to the bottom of the stairs and James held out his hand to comfort me before giving me a hug despite feeling myself shake I replied:

"I'm ok. That was just … frightening. I haven't seen him like that before. I've seen him when he's been drunk, but that was another level. Why now?"

"Stephen told me what happened. It seems that after you threw them out, he moved in with Sarah, but obviously the novelty wore off after two weeks. She then threw him out, but he had nowhere else to go except back to their parents' house. He doesn't like it because of the lectures he gets about the way he treated you. So he decided that the most mature thing to do was get drunk. We think that when he got into that state, his irrational thinking came in to play and he decided that everything was your fault because if you hadn't thrown him out, he would still have somewhere to live."

"Well, that puts me in my place and confirms what I have been thinking since that night. I was just convenient, and it was easy for him to stay here. What on earth did I ever see in him? Please tell me he hasn't always been like this."

"If he has, he has hidden it well. But rest assured, he won't be back tonight, and when he wakes up tomorrow, he is going to feel very sorry for himself. Will you be alright here tonight or do you want to come back to ours instead?"

"Honestly, I want to stay in my house, especially as I know he won't be back tonight. But I need to get through this. I know what I did was for the best, but that doesn't mean it hurts any less, especially now. I am determined to push through. I really appreciate what you and Lacy have done, and thank you for coming over tonight."

"Ok, as long as you are sure. You know where we are if you need us. Oh, and you'd better ring mum first thing in the morning to let her know what happened before the village gossip hits. Goodnight, Jane."

"I will. Thank you, James."

With that, he was gone, and I locked the house up again, checking all the windows and doors before going to where I hoped would be my relaxing haven with my lovely new bed.

I woke at seven o'clock in the morning, and although it was a little early, I knew it was probably best to ring Auntie May and let her know what had happened, because if I didn't and she heard it from someone else she would only worry.

"Morning, Jane. Are you ok? You're up early."

"I just wanted to let you know before anyone else put their spin on it … Peter came round last night, worse the wear, drunk, and making lots of noise. He wanted me to let him in. I had to get James to come, who got Peter's brother, Stephen, to take him back to their parents' house."

"Oh, darling, you should have rung us last night! Are you sure you're ok?"

"I actually am." Even I was surprised at how cool and calm I felt. "He didn't get in the house, and the worst he did was shout and bang on the door. It was frightening at the time. While James was coming round, Lacy stayed on the phone with me, which helped a lot. In a strange way, it confirmed exactly what I've been thinking over the last month, and honestly, it was a relief because it shows that I made the right decision in getting rid of him and concentrating on myself from now on."

"I am so pleased, and as long as you really are ok, then I will forgive you for not ringing us last night. I am just glad James and Lacy were there for you. Hopefully there won't be a next time, but if there is, we can help. Now, onto happier things - what are you doing today? I wondered if you wanted to go shopping."

I beamed. "I would love a day shopping! I was planning on going anyway, but as always, it will be lovely going with you. Shall I have breakfast and get ready before I come and pick you up at nine o'clock?"

"No, I tell you what. Get ready and come over, and I will get breakfast ready. That way, you won't need to do the dishes. We can leave them for your uncle to do while we are out, and we can leave whenever we are ready."

"Ha ha, ok, I will see you shortly."

Walking into my aunt and uncle's house, I noticed the table set for breakfast. Coming up to me, my uncle kissed me on the cheek and said, "You sit yourself down and I will get your coffee. Your aunt is just making your favourite pancakes for breakfast."

"Does she need a hand?"

"She said I was to tell you that she is capable of making her favourite niece breakfast without any help."

"I meant it as well," my aunt said, carrying a plate stacked with pancakes. She leaned over and, like Uncle Mike, kissed me on the cheek before sitting down opposite. "Are you sure you are alright after Peter's visit last night?"

"I really am, although your pancakes will make me feel even better."

"Of course they will! They always had magic properties."

Laughing, Uncle Mike came in with the coffees and said to my aunt. "Are you still trying to get her to believe that you make magic pancakes?"

"I don't need to get her to believe it, she knows, don't you, Jane?"

"Of course," I replied, and we all laughed together, which felt so natural and relaxed., I hadn't realised how much I needed that.

The rest of breakfast went by quickly as we talked about what my uncle was going to do after he had tidied up the breakfast dishes and while we were out spending all his "hard-earned money", as he called it. Leaving Uncle Mike with the breakfast dishes, we left to go shopping. Before we left, Uncle Mike said I wasn't allowed to let Auntie May visit the craft shop. He really did know her well, although I didn't believe he thought I was *that* strong.

It didn't take long to get to the shops, and obviously my aunt shopped till she dropped as we went into every shop and department store. Each time I tried to find out what we were looking for, she would reply with, "I will know it when I see it." By the time we had neared the craft shop, we already had quite a few bags filled with clothes for us both. We had also got close to the limit of what we could carry without our hands dropping off, so she couldn't buy too much! Well, that was what I thought; she still bought some material and some wool.

We had just got back to the car when my aunt turned to me and said, "James suggested we all met up in the pub tonight. Lacy has been working all day at an event, so he thought it would be nice if she could put her feet up and be treated to some family magic for the night. But only if that's aright with you?"

"Of course it is. I think Lacy would enjoy it, and I for one would love a night out at the pub, especially after shopping with you. I need a glass of wine to recover!"

We drove past my aunt and uncle's house to drop the car off so that we could walk to the pub as it was only five to ten minutes from out houses and it meant that my aunt could hide her purchases from the craft shop before my uncle saw them. It was the game they like to play; he didn't really mind her visiting the craft shop, but it had been a personal joke between the pair of them for years. Uncle Mike was waiting for us, so we walked towards the pub together. Now that James didn't live above the pub and was only there during the day, I know he didn't get so many chances to visit in the evenings, but I didn't realise that it would be such a wonderful night. The whole day, from breakfast through to the shopping trip, down to sitting in the pub with a lot of the people I had grown up with, all there laughing and joking among themselves, was amazing. It was the first time in a while that I actually remember thoroughly enjoying myself. I could really just be me without worrying about what I was saying or doing or even clock watching to make sure I was home in time. Seeing people now that Peter and I had broken up reinforced how much I had given up to stay in that relationship.

Just as the evening was ending, James whispered to me, "I wanted to ask you something … I asked Lacy to marry me, and she said yes, but we didn't want to announce our engagement if it was going to upset you because of your split with Peter."

"You'd better be joking! I think it's wonderful news, and don't you dare not shout it from the roof tops, especially on my behalf. What you and Lacy have is so far away from what Peter and I had, and one day, I hope to have someone who loves me as much as you two love each other. It will also be nice not being the topic for gossip for once."

"Thank you. Lacy was worried about upsetting you."

With my blessing, James stood up and went to the bar. The next thing I knew, everyone was being given a glass of champagne, and James stood on top of the bar. The perks of owning the place, I suppose. I looked over to Lacy, who was bright red, so I moved next to her and put my arm round her.

"I couldn't be happier for you," I said.

Before Lacy had a chance to respond, James called everyone to be quiet.

"Last night, I asked Lacy to marry me, and she said yes! We are engaged!"

The whole bar cheered, then the football team helped James off the bar and carried him back to where we were sitting so that everyone could congratulate the happy couple.

"Are you ok?" Auntie May asked me with a concerned frown on my face.

I thought for a minute smiling and replied, "Yes, I really am. They make an amazing couple, and I am so pleased for them."

Just then, Lacy came up to us, and after giving Auntie May a kiss on the cheek, she said she had something important to ask me in private.

"We are having an engagement party for everyone here at the pub, and although I fully understand it if you didn't want to, I would be honoured if you would sing a couple of songs for James. I know you might not feel up to it, and I really do understand that."

"Lacy, I would love to sing for you and James, just as long as you realise that I may not be as good as I used to be. It has been a long time since I last performed in front of anyone."

"Thank you! Don't be silly, you will blow everyone away. And James would love it - he's your number one fan. But I want it to be our secret as it will be my gift to him."

"That's lovely. Your secret is safe with me. Do you know what you want me to sing or do you want me to pick?"

"You can pick. We will both love anything you sing. You're a star."

"Leave it with me."

A few more people came up to congratulate Lacy and James before the evening came to a close

Later that night, I realised I had two weeks to decide what I would sing. It had been a few years since I had last sung in public, as Peter insisted that I stop singing at the few events I had regularly sung at since I was a child. Apparently, "it was embarrassing." To save arguments, I had foolishly agreed. The last time I had come off the stage I'd cried and there was no one there to offer me comfort. I hadn't told anyone it would be my last performance. I didn't want to feel my aunt and uncle's concern as I had given up something I loved. Singing gave me comfort and a connection to my mum. When Lacy asked me to sing, I couldn't believe it. I realised that I may have hidden parts of me, but I was strong enough to come through and still be me. The other consequence of Lacy asking me was that yet again I realised it was another thing I had given up for Peter without even realising. While I sat on my sofa thinking about my love of singing and all the things I had missed out on, I could feel the tears coming down my face. I was glad I was on my own as I really was an ugly crier., I wasn't even sure why I was crying. I was so mixed up inside. One minute I was feeling frustrated that I had given so much of myself away over the years, and the next I was annoyed at myself because I had ignored my family when they had pointed out what I had given up. Swiping the tears aways and trying to get rid of the anger, I let out a scream so loud I was surprised that the police weren't called. But I did feel better.

I loved singing. Lacy asking me to do this for James was such an honour, and as long as I could get back to the standard I was before I'd stopped, I might be able to see if I could restart it. I was such a fool. Singing was the one thing that I did for *me*. It relieved my stress and calmed me as soon as I got into the zone.

For the next two weeks, as well as working as a music teacher at the local school, I spent every spare minute I had singing, just to reinforce myself that I could do it, I knew I still had the voice, but I felt nervous and didn't want to let anyone down, although I knew deep down that Lacy wouldn't ask me if she didn't think I could do it. Each time I sang I felt the joy it brought me. Lacy and I decided I would sing three songs, but I had a secret for her as well because I had written a song just for the two of them, and I was going to sing that as well. It was hard writing the song. Sitting at my desk in my spare room, I went through so many pieces of paper as I scribbled.

I was putting too much pressure on writing a perfect song. I was forcing the words to come out when I knew that they should have been free to fall all by themselves. This continued for a couple of days, so I decided I needed to leave it for a while. While I was at work I remembered that in my loft was my old song writing folder. I needed a refresher, and that would be the best place to look. I hadn't been in the loft for a while and I knew it would be hard being up there because I had a lot of my mum's things in there, things that I couldn't bear to part with. After finding the right box, I spent over an hour sitting on the loft floor going through my old books. I was just about to leave the loft when something caught my eyes. Sitting on the top of one of mum's boxes lay a photo album. I don't know why it was there because I thought I had kept all her albums downstairs, so I took it with me. Pouring myself a glass of wine, I went into the living room and started to go through the photo album, which had pictures of me, mum, Aunt May, and Uncle Mike with a cute-looking James. These were photos that I hadn't seen for a while. and it really hit me how much love there was between us. It was at that moment inspiration struck. Running to my office, I wrote James and Lacy's love song in one sitting. The next two weeks went by quickly. I had gone out shopping with Lacy and Auntie May and had rearranged my house. With work and singing practice, I was busy, but for the first time in a long time, I was enjoying myself. The icing on the cake was that I hadn't heard from Peter at all.

When the day of the engagement party arrived, I rehearsed at home to keep it all a secret. Walking into the pub, I couldn't believe how many people were there! It seemed that all of Lacy's family had come, as well as the rest of the whole village. I doubt there was anyone left in the village that night. The lovely thing about James' pub was that it really was the heart of the village. It took me ages to get a drink. I wasn't drinking alcohol because of my singing, but I could feel the nerves seeping in. Moving towards the bar was slow progress as I was stopped by everyone wanting to talk to me. I was just thinking about leaving the pub and going round the back way into the pub to try and avoid the crowds, when I got a text from my uncle.

"I have a glass of water for you at our table. We are at the back of the pub if you want to join us."

"Thank you, on my way," I replied. Making my way towards the back of the pub was easier than trying to get to the bar, although there were still a lot of people. Sitting at a large table, I found all my family and Lily and Lacy's family. The happy couple were nowhere to be seen. Apparently, they were stuck in amongst all the people. After saying hello to everyone on the table, I sat down next to my aunt.

"I didn't expect this many people."

"No one did. James is holding on to Lacy so she doesn't get lost in the crush of people. I'm glad we got here early to help set things up, otherwise I think we would have struggled to get a table," my aunt responded.

Looking around the pub, I saw a section of the room had a little stage put up and a table on the stage set with white tablecloths. People started to crowd our table as our neighbours descended on us. After drinking my water, I needed some fresh air, so trying to get up from the table, I walked towards the door when I heard Lacy call my name. I waited as she managed to work her way through the crowds.

"Jane, sorry, we haven't caught up with you yet."

Leaning over I gave her a kiss and cuddle. "Don't be silly, your fan club awaits."

"I know, it's mad! But it should settle down as food will be served, and then as long as you are sure you will be alright to sing after the buffet is over, James will do a little speech and then you can take over the microphone and sing then."

"I can't wait. I was just going to get some fresh air. Where is James, anyway? I was told he had you firmly in his hand so you didn't get lost?"

"He did, but I persuaded him that he needed to get the food going so everything can calm down a bit now that most people seem to be here."

"Good idea."

"Why don't you pop out the back way to get some fresh air? I have made up some little platters for the family table so that we don't need to join the queue for food, although don't be too long, my brother Danny is there."

"I won't. I will see you shortly."

I needed some fresh air because I was feeling a little apprehensive, but I was looking forward to singing again, especially for my biggest fans.

Once I had calmed my nerves down a bit outside, I went back to the family table to find that, true to her word, Lacy had put some individual platters on our table. I was so glad that they had decided to have a buffet so I didn't need to eat a full three-course meal right before I sang. It didn't take long for the platters to be emptied, and even the buffet table on the stage had some food left. I think Danny spotted that because he excused himself from the table to go and help the staff out. Looking over at the table, we realised him 'helping them out' meant making sure no food was left.

The tables were removed, and the small local band took their places. I had worked with these people before and had already given them my music. With everyone in there right place, James took to the stage and started his "Thank you for coming" speech. The next thing I knew, James had done his speech and left the stage. Taking a deep breath to try to calm myself down, I grabbed the microphone, took another deep breath, and walked on stage.

"Hi, I won't keep you long, but I was asked by the new fiancée for a favour, and we all know how rarely that happens! This is for you, James, from Lacy."

Giving the band a small nod, the music started playing, and I got into my familiar zone. I started off with Belinda Carlisle's song, We Want the Same Thing, followed by Eternal Flame from the Bangles. Frank Sinatra's I Got You Under My Skin was the third song. I calmed my nerves by focussing on looking at the clock in the distance, letting the music run through my body, and in no time I could feel myself moving to the music. It was as if I hadn't had any time off. During the songs I could remember my mother's joy at my singing, The place singing took me to where I was safe and protected and what I had missed when I had bowed down to Peter's pressure. When I looked out at the audience and saw that there sole focus was on me and they were enchanted, this gave me a feeling of empowerment, I was home and back in my happy place. by the time I got to the finale and the song I had written for them, called Magic Love. I was so emotional, and to try to stop the tears from leaking, I closed my eyes. After I had finished, I looked up and everyone had tears in their eyes. The temptation to escape from the stage was strong. All my emotions on display made me feel so vulnerable. But I finished the song and calmly thanked everyone for listening. I then made a quick getaway, only to be caught by James and Lacy.

"Wow. Thank you so much! Your voice is amazing as always," said James. "I can't believe Lacy talked you into that, but I am very glad that she did. That is the best gift I have had in a long time; I have missed hearing you sing."

Holding back from showing too much of the emotional turmoil I was going through, I couldn't say much, but I managed to respond with a quick thank you. Knowing that I wasn't going to get away as quickly as I hoped, I was relieved when Lacy handed me a much-needed glass of wine, which I took a gulp from before Lacy continued.

"Jane, thank you so much. The song you wrote us was beautiful and so unexpected."

"No problem, and I know you didn't want any engagement gifts, but I got this made for you. It's the words of the song I wrote framed with pictures of the pair of you together."

Before I got on the stage, I managed to ask one of the staff behind the bar to look after the large frame I got for them and when I had finished he put it by the side of the stage so that it was close at hand. I handed them the picture I had made up for them. Lacy burst out crying and James pulled the pair of us in for a hug. He was equally as speechless, which is something I never thought I would see. We were just managing to pull ourselves together when Auntie May and Uncle Mike came over.

"I have said it before and I will say it again - you have the voice of an angel! I can't believe you kept that a secret. I could have been prepared and bought a year's supply of tissues. Instead, I had to use Mike's handkerchief. Although there is nothing more comforting to me than Mike's hankies when I am crying."

"Ha ha, that is very true. Next time, I promise I will warn you – if there *is* a next time."

"Of course there will be a next time! You didn't see everyone as soon as you sang that first line. You couldn't hear a pin drop, and before you had finished, there wasn't a dry eye in the place. Even the men had tears in their eyes."

Looking very proud, Uncle Mike said, "That's because my niece can reach anyone with her wonderful voice."

Speechless, I managed to splutter, "Thanks, Uncle Mike," and gave him a big hug, which he reciprocated. I beamed, a feeling of warmth spreading through my heart, which, judging by the smile on my uncle's face, was visible on the outside as much as I could feel it on the inside. I was back in my happy place: singing.

Chapter 3

David

I had walked into James' engagement party with the view that I would just stop long enough to say congratulations and have one drink. I'd known James since we'd been to university together, and it was he who had persuaded me to open my restaurant, Fish by the River, here in Greengrove after my divorce came through, and for that, I owe him. It was one of the best decisions I have ever made. Since opening the restaurant, I'd hardly had any time off work, but I'd promised James I would show my face, despite my exhaustion. What I really needed was an early night.

I was just finishing off my drink after toasting the happy couple when I spotted a gorgeous woman with long mousy hair, wearing the most striking blue dress. As she took the microphone off James, who looked a bit confused, I noticed a flicker of fear pass through her eyes. I wasn't really listening to what she was saying. I was too busy looking at her. The next thing I knew, she started singing, and I'm pretty sure I stopped breathing. I couldn't tear my eyes away or make a sound. I didn't want to miss one moment of her performance.

She sang four different songs, three of which I had heard

before, but never as beautiful and with such emotion. The fourth song was not one I had heard of. As soon as she finished, she opened her eyes, smiled, and walked off the stage.

My eyes followed her, and my heart began to beat in my chest. *What is happening to me?* I took a deep breath.

Just as I put my empty glass on the bar, I saw James and Lacy hug the singer and talk to her. Then James' mum and dad greeted her as well. She was obviously well known to the family and not someone hired for the night. The bar staff were returning back behind the bar when I overheard them talk about the singer.

"Did you know she had that in her?"

"No clue. I've known her all my life and I didn't realise she could sing like that. I mean, she use to sing at school concerts, but not like that."

"I'm not sure I'll like any other versions of those songs after hearing her tonight. Not even the originals. Just think how lucky the kids in her school are having her as their music teacher."

Although I still didn't know who she was, I knew a few more things about her: she was a teacher and obviously came from the village. I decided now was the time to congratulate James and Lacy on their engagement, especially while the mousy-haired woman was still around.

With trepidation and the hope that I would get to meet the singer, I walked up to the happy couple.

"Congratulations, James, and of course you too, Lacy. I hope you know what you are doing. James can be a bit of a handful."

Laughing, James replied, "No more than you, David! I did learn everything from you, after all."

"Oh, come off it, James, we have to be honest. We taught each other."

"That's true. David, I would like to introduce you to my cousin, Jane. She's a music teacher at the local school."

My heart skipped a beat. "A name to the wonderful singing voice. I have to say, it is a pleasure to meet you. I don't think I've ever seen such a riveted audience. We were all stunned into silence! You really know how to blow people away."

With rosy cheeks. she replied, "Thank you. I'm glad you enjoyed it." Then she looked away from me as if she didn't trust the compliment.

I turned to James' mum and dad and said, "Hello, Mike and May. Long-time no see. When are you going to come to the restaurant for dinner? I've nearly been here a year and you haven't visited yet."

"Well, if you weren't so busy, we would be able to get a table."

"You know I would always find a table for you. If it wasn't for your son, I wouldn't have had a restaurant here, so I owe him, and in turn I owe you, especially after the big welcome I was given. Not to mention staying at your house until I could find a place."

"Don't mention it. You owe us nothing. Although saying that, I would love to visit your restaurant. Actually, while I think of it, it's your birthday next week, Jane. If you have nothing planned and David can fit us all in, we could go for dinner there next Friday night to celebrate."

Everyone agreed that they were free, so I excused myself after checking how many people they needed the table for. I then phoned the restaurant.

"No, the place hasn't burnt down," my front of house manager replied.

"Really, Rebecca, is that anyway to answer the phone?" I chuckled. "Is the private room booked out next Friday?"

"No, it's free both Thursday and Friday."

"That's great. Can you book it out for me in the name of Jameson, but put me down as the point of contact, and it's for a table of six."

"Of course, no problem. I have done that for you."

"Great, thanks. Is everything ok there or do you need me back?"

"Everything is fine. I knew you were going to ask. I told you when you left that you deserve the night off."

"Ok but any problems please ring me."

"I won't. Now go away, boss. Some of us are busy."

Rebecca had been my friend since I'd gone to university. As soon as I had moved to Greengrove, she had decided to come with me. Our relationship was more like a brother and sister, maybe because she used to be my sister-in-law. Sometimes she could be just a little bit cheeky and bossy, but she was doing an excellent job as the front of house manager, so I couldn't complain.

"Right, everyone, you are all booked in for next Friday. So now, May, you have no excuse."

"I'm looking forward to it."

James and Lacy excused themselves to chat to other well-wishers, which left me, Jane, Mike, and May to discuss forthcoming local events, including the autumn fair, which was due to happen next month.

As time was getting on and it was almost eleven o'clock,

people started to leave the pub. A good number of them stopped to tell Jane how wonderful her songs were and how they hoped she would be doing more singing. Mike and May offered her a lift home, but she said she was quite happy walking. Although it was October, for once, it wasn't raining or too cold. I promised them I would make sure Jane got home safely as I was walking home as well. With that, they kissed her on the cheek and left.

"Thank you for reassuring them, but you really don't need to worry. I will be ok walking back. It's not that far."

"It's not a problem to escort a beautiful lady home. I would never forgive myself if I didn't see it through."

"Ok then, who am I to turn down such an offer?"

"At least I will know you have arrived safely at your door. Do you have a coat?"

"Yes, it's the red one over by the table near James and Lacy."

"That's perfect. We can say goodbye to them on the way."

After saying goodbye, we left, and although I knew Jane was right and it wasn't too far to walk, it was nice managing to chat with her one on one.

"I know I have said it already, but you have a beautiful singing voice. Your range and style are far reaching; James says you are a music teacher, but do you sing professionally as well?"

"I haven't done any professional singing for a few years now, but I used to. When Lacy asked me to sing for James, I was a little bit nervous, but then I remembered how much I love it. This is my second year teaching. It's a good job."

With Jane navigating to her house, we reached it in no time at all.

"Here you are, safely delivered home."

"Do you want to come in for a coffee?"

"Thank you for the offer, but I'd better be going, I have to be up early tomorrow. It was lovely to meet you. Would it be possible to take a rain check?"

I really wanted to go in for a coffee, but I thought after tonight she would be tired, and I needed time to think. Jane was the first person since my divorce that I had been interested in, and because of her connection to James, I didn't want to put a foot wrong. I wanted to take this slow so that I didn't make the mistakes with Jane that I had made in previous relationships. I have never been one for lots of casual relationships. I needed to feel connected, both mentally and physically, with my partner.

"It was lovely to meet you too, David. I would like that."

I watched her go inside her house and turn her lights on.

Before she closed the front door, she turned around and smiled.

During the walk back to my house, which wasn't that far away from Jane's, I realised that I hadn't really had time to get myself familiar with the village, but now that the restaurant was up and running, that was going to change. One of the most important things about running a business in a small village is getting to know the people who live in the area, and that was one of the things I had struggled to do since moving here as I had been so busy getting the restaurant up and running.

Turning in for the night, it was really hard to get the image and voice of Jane out of my head. I had never heard anything as beautiful as that, and the effect it had on the room was definitely one I had never felt or been affected by before. Talking to her, I realised that she was just as genuine as James and his parents. I really would like to get to know her better.

As far as I could tell, she was nothing like Stephanie, my ex-wife.

Jane

Wow, what a night! That could not have gone better, and I really enjoyed singing. It just reinforced how much I had unwittingly given up for Peter. On the flip side, it also reinforced that I was never again going to let any man persuade me to give things up that I love.

Lacy and James had a really good turnout. In fact, I think the whole village was there. It was great seeing people I hadn't seen for a long time. A few people said they were glad that Peter and I had broken up, but they were not happy about the way it had happened. It appears a lot of people hadn't bought into his act as much as I had.

One of the surprises of the night was meeting James' friend, David. James had talked about him before, so I knew he owned his own restaurant and that he'd moved here after finishing university, where he'd met James. I wasn't interested in another relationship, especially as it has only been just a few months since I'd called my engagement off, but there was just something about David. When he shook hands with me, it was like I was being given an electric shock. The way he laughed and joked with my aunt and uncle and James - this man was full of self-confidence and personal awareness. What you see is what you get. The walk back to my house was one of the most relaxing walks I'd ever had with a man. We talked about our work and my singing and the village. True to his word, he didn't make things uncomfortable when we got back to mine. He didn't move in for a kiss when we got to the doorstep, he just walked back so I could unlock the door. He then told me it was nice meeting me and waited until I was safely in before he left. After being with Peter, it was good to see that there were still some real gentlemen out there.

It was difficult trying to get to sleep that night because I was still on a high after my performance. In the end, I got out of bed and decided I would work on a plan to reinstate my business as a singer. The more I thought about it, the more I liked the idea. Now was the time to do something for *me*. In the morning, I would talk to Lacy about going on her events books so that if she had anyone wanting a singer, they could contact me. One of the things I needed to do was organise a demo so that I could download it to my website for people to hear. A few of my musician friends had told me how important it was to be on social media. Word of mouth was also a good way to get your name out there. But I wanted to start this off slowly because I loved my teaching job and I didn't want this to take over. A few gigs a month would be good, but if I didn't have any, it wouldn't be a worry.

It was four o'clock in the morning, and now that my brain had been emptied of all the things going round it, I was starting to feel tired, so I decided to go back to bed. I didn't have anything planned for the next day, except Auntie May's barbeque, but that wasn't until the evening. Now that everything had quietened down in my head, sleeping was quite easy.

Until I was awoken by my doorbell. With a start, I looked over to the clock. It was 10:30. Thinking it was the postman, I put my robe on and quickly went to answer the door. To my shock, it was Peter. He was standing there in his normal cocky manor. What had I seen in him?

"What do you want?" I snapped.

"I want to talk to you. Would it possible for me to come in? I really dislike talking on the doorstep. It's so common."

"I don't think I have anything to say to you. But fine. You've got no more than five minutes. That should give you enough time to say your piece. Then you will leave." I opened the door wide so that he could come in. Luckily, I had grabbed my phone, and I quickly texted James to let him know that Peter was in my house. Just to be safe. Peter had never hurt me before, but the man who'd showed up at my door last time was not the man I remembered, and I wasn't prepared to take the risk. By the time I walked into the living room, he had already taken a seat on the sofa.

"I see you have decorated and changed a few things around. It's very floral and … a bit gross, to be honest."

"Well, I didn't do it for you." I really was trying to stay calm, but seriously, who did he think he was? "Say what you have to say because the clock is ticking, and you only have three minutes left," I replied, hands on my hips.

"Why are you being like this? It's not you."

"Tick tock."

"Obviously you are PMSing. Maybe I should come back next week when you are over it."

His cheek was amazing. Oh, to have that ego. *I bet he doesn't get away with that round his mother*, I thought to myself.

"As soon as you walk out that door in two minutes time, I never want to see you again."

"Jane, come on, darling. I came here to apologise that you found me in bed with Sarah. I didn't mean for it to happen, and I regretted it as soon as I left your house. I need you, and I want you back."

I wondered if he could see the steam coming out of my ears. *Deep breath and count to ten*, I repeated to myself, wondering if I might need a higher number.

"You actually only apologised for being caught. You didn't apologise that you were and obviously having sex with her during our relationship. As for you wanting me back, that's not going to happen. Time's up. You need to leave."

"Oh, Jane, please don't be difficult. If I move in again, we can go back to the way we were, and I will even try to live with the new decorations. But please let me come back."

I had heard enough, so I stood and turned around,

glaring at him. "When I was growing up, I used to hear parents say to their children, N O spells no, and I used to think 'what an odd saying'. But I now know why they say it when people just don't listen. So here goes: Peter, N O spells NO. Now I have made that clear, get out."

He huffed and stood up, then walked towards the door and said, "I'm not giving up. I will be back." Just as he opened the front door, James was standing there with his spare key in the lock as if he was about to open the door.

In a sulky manner, Peter turned round and said to James, "Might have known you would show up. Are you now her bodyguard or something?"

James laughed and said, "Something!"

Peter pushed past him, then turned and said to me, "I will see you soon."

"I hope not," I replied as I watched him get into his car.

James came into the house and went straight to the kitchen. Putting the kettle on, he asked, "Do you want a drink?"

"Yes please - a coffee would be great. I'll go get dressed."

Ready for the day, I walked into the living room to find James sitting in front of the television, watching the football. "You know I was joking when I said that you seemed quite at home, but seeing you like this makes me wonder if I have walked into the right house."

With an apologetic smile, he said, "I thought you were going to take ages getting ready, so I thought I would make myself comfortable. But now you're here I can turn it off and you can tell me what the loser was doing here." I replayed the story of Peter's intrusion, and James' view was exactly the same as mine.

"Oh, so he wants to move in with you because he doesn't have anywhere else to live. Please tell me you told him where to go."

"Trust me, I did, but he seems to only hear what he wants to. At least he was sober this time. Anyway, thank you for coming again. I just didn't know what he wanted and whether he would actually go when I told him to."

Knocking my arm with his, James said, "Any time," and we drank our coffee while discussing what we were going to do today. When James heard that I had no plans, he suggested I spend the day with him and Lacy down by the river. They were having a picnic lunch. I tried to tell him that I didn't want to intrude, but he was having none of it and even suggested that if I made some of my cookies and brought them along, it wouldn't hurt. He then suggested that he would even help me make them, so that was what we did. It reminded me of when we were at primary school; his mum would pick us up because my mum was working, and we'd make cookies for our pudding.

Having finished in the kitchen and tidied up while the cookies cooled, I set about making a jug of peach iced tea to take along with us as it was an unusually hot day. After packing a bag with sunscreen, an extra blanket, the iced tea, and the all-important cookies, James and I went to pick Lacy up.

The walk to the river was lovely and calming. We saw a few of the people from the village out and about working on their gardens. I couldn't remember when I had last taken a walk down the river. I knew it wasn't in the last four years as Peter had hated going out for walks, and when he was free, he didn't like me doing anything or booking anything that he didn't want to do.

As we walked along the riverbank, I saw a stone bench set back a little from the riverbank.

"Wow, look at this wonderful seat! It looks like it's shaped like a sofa. I never knew it was here."

"It's my special place," Lacy replied. "I used to come here when I wanted to be on my own and when I was hiding from Sarah. Although I came here when things were bad, it was also my thinking place. This is where James asked me to marry him."

I never knew my cousin was such a romantic, but it was obvious that the connection he felt for Lacy knew no bounds.

The best place for a picnic was beside one of the village's oldest bridges, which reached over the river's glistening water. It was set back a little bit from the river so that we weren't in anyone's way when they were walking past. We sat underneath a tall oak tree, having placed the red tartan blanket on the grass. The tree provided some shade from the hot sun, and in front of us we had the river. Behind us was a huge hill, upon which we could only just see the remains of St Catherine's Church. There was something familiar about this place, watching the Ducks swimming by with a line of ducklings in their wake. I smiled and sighed as the sun warmed my face. Lacy began laying out our little feast of cheese sandwiches, ham quiche, crisps, and of course our cookies and peach iced tea. I realised that this was the place my mum used to bring James and I and a few of our friends on weekends. We used to race up to the top of the hill. It was normally the boys that ran because my friends and I were too busy trying to make daisy chains. That memory must have bought a smile to my face because James noticed and asked why I was grinning like a Cheshire cat.

"I was just remembering when mum used to bring us all here and you and your friends would have competitions running up the hill, and Heidi and I used to sit and make daisy chains. I think we were about six years old. Do you remember?"

"Yes, I do. What happened to Heidi?"

"Heidi moved back to France just after we finished school in July when she was seven. Do you wish sometimes you could go back to that age and tell yourself to do things differently?"

"Damn, I forgot you have a really good memory! But would you really want to go back to when you were young? Yes, there are some things that may have been easier back then, but other things were a lot harder. I think the problem is that when we look at our life there are things that we wish we had done differently; it's not that we *should have* done them differently, but it's a case of realising when you're older that there were other ways of doing things when you were younger."

"Who knew you could be so insightful? I guess you're right; It's not necessarily my childhood that I would change, it's just I think I am still upset – no, maybe annoyed – that I wasted so much time on Peter. I started going out with him when I was still at school, and overtime I gave up so many things without realising."

Just at that moment, Lacy, who had been setting out the food, leaned over, gave me a hug, and told me to stop thinking of it that way. I needed to just put Peter out of my mind and concentrate on the future, *my* future.

After sitting, talking, and eating for an hour, James decided it was time for us to recreate our run up the hill with Lacy as referee. Despite him cheating at the bottom by trying to hold me back, he still didn't win. It was really fun doing something as silly as running up the hill. By the time I got to the top of the hill, I was laughing and I felt as if I didn't have a care in the world. I remembered the wonderful view from up here, so while James was doubled over with a stitch, I stood looking out over Greengrove, feeling free. Coming down was difficult because my legs were so sore I could feel every painful movement, but at least I ran more gracefully than James, who tripped up and ended up rolling down the hill. He then tried to class that as a victory as he was the quickest to the bottom. I had forgotten what being out with James was like. I'd forgotten what having fun was like. It was then that I remembered that we never used to come down this way. We used to zigzag down and go a different way, which wasn't such a quick drop; it was more of a steady walk.

Pushing me over, James said, "You're right. I remember when you worked that out. It made it easier going down without getting bruises and holes in our trouser legs."

After recovering from the race, we packed up the remains of the picnic and started walking back to their house to refresh, and then we were off to Auntie May's for her barbeque.

Every Saturday, she'd have a family event, but once in a while, she'd invite almost everyone she knew. They normally ended up being about once a month. I asked her once why she went to so much trouble, and she replied, "It is good for everyone in the village to get together and for those who are on their own to know that they still have friends and something to look forward to. It was nice seeing everyone again, and throughout the night, people were still congratulating me on my singing from the night before.

It was during this time that I heard a man's voice say, "I told you last night that you were amazing and should sing more." I turned around, and David was standing there, holding a bottle of beer with a smile on his face.

Turning round to face him, I replied, "Hello, David, I'm so glad you came." I had never seen him at the barbeques before, although I knew he had always been invited. James and Auntie May were worried that he had been working too hard. On the walk home last night, we'd had a lovely chat, and I mentioned that if he came today I would introduce him to people he didn't know. Despite living here for a while, he hadn't really met any of the locals as he had been busy getting the restaurant off the ground, and from everything I'd heard, he had definitely succeeded in doing that.

After doing a circuit of everyone, we made it back to

James and Lacy. As the men chatted amongst themselves, Lacy and I wandered off to talk to Lily about the community centre and some of the upcoming events they had planned.

"Lily, I was thinking about the choir we use to have, and I thought I would ask if you thought the community centre would like to host it again, because I don't mind running it."

"That would be wonderful! I know some people that would love for it to be restarted, and I can't think of anyone better to organise it than you."

"Why don't we have an open night where anyone who is interested can come along so we can gauge interest?"

Lily got her diary out and sorted out a date for a couple weeks' time.

"Why don't we have the first event on a Sunday, then we can see what people's availability is from there,"

James and David came over with a plate of food for both Lacy and me.

"If you would excuse us, Lily, it's about time these wonderful women ate something."

"Of course, James. I will sort that out for you, Jane, and ring you later."

With our plates we walked over to the spare table. James asked, "What are you looking so excited about?"

Lacy was practically vibrating with excitement. "Jane is going to reform the community centre choir; it's going to be really good, and soon the choir will be able to entre competitions like they used to."

"I don't know about entering competitions, but Lily agreed that it would be good to have the choir back, and I would love to organise it."

While James and Lacy were talking, she tried to persuade him to join the choir. David whispered to me, "I hope it was ok me getting you some food. James helped me with the buffet choices, but I didn't want to turn up empty-handed with no food for you whilst everyone else was eating."

"This is lovely, thank you. I couldn't have picked better myself. I normally stand in front of the table for ages deciding what I want."

I was thinking that I didn't ever remember a time when Peter had got a plate of food for me. I remembered doing it for him a few times, and normally then he would moan about me putting something on his plate he didn't want. Maybe it was unfair to keep comparing him to other people, but it seemed that my mind just kept telling me, 'I told you he wasn't for you.'

After a lovely dinner and helping Auntie May clear up, I excused myself to go home when David shouted my name. "Are you off home? I can walk with you if you like?" It was at that moment that I realised I hadn't been home since this morning's conversation with Peter, and the more I thought about it, the more worried I was that he was just going to keep turning up until he got what he wanted. Although I knew it was weak and I should not let Peter change my behaviour, I decided that I would take David up on his offer, so like the night before, we had a leisurely walk back to my house.

Chapter 4

David

I was sitting down, talking to James and Lacy, when James' mum came up to talk to him. I was trying not to eavesdrop, but as soon as I heard Jane's name mentioned, my ears opened up.

"James, I'm worried about Jane. I know she looks relaxed, but I can tell that there is something bothering her."

"I think it's Peter. She sent me a text this morning telling me that Peter was visiting unannounced, so I went round there, and when I got there, she was trying to usher him out of the house."

Listening to this, I started to become worried about Jane as well. "Is Peter dangerous?" I asked.

"Not that we know," James replied. "He can be verbally angry when he's been drinking, and he seems to think he can do no wrong and that everyone is there for his benefit, especially Jane. But as far as we know, he hasn't been physically abusive. But I don't like the way he is treating Jane. It's as if he wants her back for the convenience of being with her. But she won't go back. He betrayed her ... I think she has realised what we all knew; that Peter wasn't the right man for her. He was stifling her."

"I'm worried about her, not only because I think James is right, but also I think she has realised how much of herself she gave up so now she is taking on too much."

To me it seemed she was just trying to regain her independence. However, I could understand why May was worried about her taking on too much. M first impressions of Jane were that she seemed so strong, but the more I thought about it, the more I realised there was a little bit of her that needed reassurance that she was doing things right.

"I think it might be a good idea if someone walks Jane home tonight, just in case Peter is hanging around trying to talk to her again."

"I would like to help," I told them.

"I think that's a good idea, don't you, James? We don't want Jane to think we are babying her and not trusting her on her own."

For the second night running, I found myself walking home with Jane, and just like the previous night, it was another relaxing walk. When we reached her house, she asked me if I wanted to come in for a coffee, and I accepted this time. I hadn't felt this comfortable with any woman since my divorce. My ex-wife turned out to be one of the worst mistakes in my life, and I'm glad I realised what she was doing and who she was doing it with before it was too late. We had only been married a year before I called a stop to it. Although the marriage was difficult, I had always thought she loved me, but when she accidentally sent me a text message to me instead her lover, I realised the truth, especially when she described me as 'a waste of space'. The confrontation from that message was interesting, especially as she showed no remorse, so I decided that I wouldn't waste my time anymore. I had already wasted enough. Leaving her was one of the best things I had ever done.

As soon as Jane opened her front door, we walked in, but she seemed nervous.

"Are you ok?" I asked.

"Oh, yes, sorry. The last person I invited in told me the room was very floral, so I was worried it would be too feminine for you. I mean, we could sit outside, but it's a bit cold."

Before she continued, I touched her elbow and said, "Jane, breathe. I think it's lovely in here. It isn't too floral, and even if it is, it's your house and it can be decorated the way you want, and visitors shouldn't say negative things about your house."

She looked at me and said, "Yes, you're right, sorry. What can I get you to drink?"

"Do you have decaf coffee or tea? I don't want to be up all

night, and I have work tomorrow. This weekend has been the first I have taken off since we opened."

"You're in luck!" she responded. "I have decaf coffee. I got it in for James as I tend to just drink peppermint tea after my two cups of real coffee in the morning."

"That's great. I will just have it black with no sugar. Do you need a hand?"

"No, that's ok. I won't be long. You sit down and relax."

She then went into the kitchen and left me wondering who would be so rude as to visit someone's house and insult the decoration. Then I remembered she said it was the last person she had invited into her house, and I knew James had been here. But it wouldn't have been him. He'd said her ex had been in her house. I bet it was him who had said it.

Nobody has the right to make people second guess themselves, especially about something as individual as how they decorate their own home. Sitting on the sofa I could see outside the living room window, where the streetlights managed to show the outline of rose bushes which were positioned close to the window. I had walked past her house on previous occasion when I had walked to work and I had admired her garden then although I didn't know who it belonged to. When she returned with the coffee, she chose to sit next to me, which made me happy, as I had been sure she was going to put distance between us and choose one of the other chairs.

"This is a lovely place. Have you lived here long?" I asked. There was something about Jane that made my protective genes well up inside me.

Smiling at me as if my comment about her house was one of the best things she had ever heard, she said, "I've lived here all my life. When my mum died, she left it to me. I love it here, and I can't think of anywhere else I want to live."

"I'm sorry about your mum, but I agree with you, it is lovely here and nice and peaceful. Your roses in the garden are some of the best I have seen for a long time. I don't have much of a garden, and what I do have is just grass. Because of the amount of time I spend at the restaurant, I pay Joe to mow the lawn and tidy it up for me, so I envy you."

"Thank you again, but I can't take credit for the garden and the roses. Mum planted them years ago, and like you, I pay Joe to take care of it all, and I wouldn't replace him or do it myself because I am more likely to kill them than keep them alive. I'm not very green-fingered. It doesn't matter how much Auntie May tries to teach me, they look at me and die."

I chuckled. "Maybe they know they can't compete with

such beauty, so they give up." As soon as I said it, I realised how corny it was. Embarrassed, I looked up only to find her laughing, and it took a little time for her to be able to keep a straight face. "Don't say a word. I know how awful that sounded, but it was worth it to see you laugh like that. I don't think I have ever seen anything so beautiful."

"Stop making me laugh! Did you swallow a book of pick up lines?" she replied, trying to hold it together without laughing again.

I don't know what came over me. I never knew I had the ability to say such sickly-sweet things. Then I did the only thing I could do in that situation. I started laughing as well, which set her off laughing even more. In the end, we were both doubled up in hysterics on the sofa. When we eventually calmed down, we managed to drink our coffee, and I was just about to get up to leave when her doorbell rang, one long, continuous noise, like they weren't taking their finger off the button.

"I'm really sorry. I'd better see who that is." She got up, but I could see the tension in her body as she looked through the peephole and then mumbled, "Oh, great."

"Are you ok?" I called to her.

"Hopefully," came back the reply, so I geared myself up

to be ready to help her. But I wanted to make sure she knew she could handle whatever or whoever it was at the door, although I had a guess.

Listening in on the conversation as she opened the door, I deduced that I was right. It was her ex-fiancé. I couldn't hear what Jane was saying, but he was being loud. I think it had something to do with the drink he had obviously had. In the end, I decided to text James just to let him know what was happening.

"Hi, sorry it's so late. I am at Jane's, and I was just getting up to leave when her ex came to the door. It appears that, by the sound of him, he is drunk."

I didn't have long to wait before James replied. "Thanks for letting me know. Would you be able to stay there for a while? I will try to get hold of his brother so that he can come and get him. I don't want Jane left on her own with him."

"No problem. I'll be here as long as she needs me."

I wasn't sure whether I should reveal myself or if that would make things worse.

Just when I had decided that I would wait, I heard her shout, "David, can you come here please?" In a flash, I was by her side. "Peter, I would like you to meet David. He is here because, unlike you, I invited him in. I would like you to go now. We are *not* getting back together. I have no desire to see you ever again, so please leave." Just as she finished her rant, another man turned up and said to Jane, "I am really sorry, Jane. I will get him out of here and try to instil in him that he is not to come around again."

"Thank you, Stephen, I really appreciate it. When he sobers up, tell him that if he keeps coming round here, I will phone the police. I just want him to leave me alone."

With a nod, the man she'd called Stephen managed to get Peter into his car and left. Jane was shaking, and I don't think it was because she was cold, so I grabbed hold of her, shut the door, and moved her into the living room. After sitting her down, I put the blanket that was on the back of the sofa around her till I got her a stiff drink. Luckily, she had her alcohol cabinet in full view, so I didn't need to go searching through cupboards. I poured her a shot of whisky and gave it to her. After a short while, she slowly drank it/

"I'm really sorry that you got involved in my drama."

"I'm not. I'm glad I was here for you. I don't mind, but I do want to let James know what happened".

"Thank you, I'm not sure I could bare to talk to him at the moment."

I was surprised by this because I thought she would have wanted to keep it quiet because she was so private. In a way this reassured me as well because at least she was being honest with James about what was happening. I suggested that she ring James just to reassure him that she was ok, which she did. She told James she was quite happy to stay in her own home tonight and that she would talk to him tomorrow.

I needed to talk to her about tonight's events but was worried how to start the conversation. "Jane," I said at the same time she said, "David." We both laughed. "Sorry, you go on," I told her.

"I just want to apologise again for tonight. I didn't expect him to turn up, especially after I saw him earlier this morning and had to listen to what he had to say. It seems that although I didn't accept him back, he isn't going to leave me alone. The thing with Peter is that he always seems to get his own way. But it's not happening this time."

"Has he always been like that?"

"Not all the time. A few times a year he would drink a lot and then he would be belligerent, but not violent. But since I threw him out of the house, he has been around a lot, insisting I get back with him."

"Is that why you split up with him?"

"Oh no, I didn't realise these things until we split up. I'm surprised you haven't heard about it. I came back from James and Lacy's moving-in-together party early and found him in my bed with someone we went to school with. I don't know if you know her – Sarah."

"Wow, no wonder you threw him out and don't want him back. Isn't she the one who used to make Lacy's life a misery?"

"Yes, that's her. I'm not sure if it was the first time he slept with someone else, and I didn't really care. I decided that it wasn't the type of relationship I wanted to be in, and since then I have realised how much I gave up to be with him without realising it. I want to be in an equal relationship with trust."

"I know how you feel. I was married a few years ago to a woman I met at university. Her name was Stephanie. But one day, I received a text that was meant for her boyfriend. It appeared that she had been in another relationship for about a year, even after we got married. He knew about me, but I didn't know about him. In the text she was moaning about me and telling him I was a waste of space. That kind of deception takes a while to get over. But eventually it hurts less and you begin to realise that a weight has been lifted off you."

"That is a great description of it. I really do feel lighter and that I am free to make my own decisions without worrying about what Peter might say or do. That is until he shows up again. But all that does is reinforce what an idiot I was to believe I meant anything to him."

"You're not an idiot. I believe people like Peter and my ex are just good at conning people for their own good, and they're the idiots because they can't see what's in front of them. We are the genuine ones, and we can't let them change who we are."

"I never looked at it that way. I guess you have been where I am now, so I will try to remember those words. Thank you."

Jane yawned, and I said to her, "It's getting late. Are you sure you're ok staying here on your own tonight? I can take you to your aunt's or James' if you like?"

"Oh no, I'm, ok now. Thank you, David. I really appreciate you staying, but he won't be back tonight. You're right, it is late, and I have a long day ahead of me tomorrow. Knowing you're here has been a great comfort. I can't thank you enough."

"No problem. If I give you my phone number, you can ring me if you have any other problems I can help with."

Jane

We exchanged numbers and then David left, and for the first time in a long time I didn't feel so alone. I knew I could always call James, but from what David said, he knew what it felt like to go through this. Although I still had no idea of the depth of Peter's problems, I knew it wasn't my fault. I double-checked that the door was locked and went to bed, knowing that sleep would take a while no matter how tired I was because my brain was whirring.

Chapter 5

Jane

It had been a busy Monday at school as it was the beginning of the new term. The kids were all excited and restless because they were catching up with the friends they hadn't seen for a few weeks. Being the music teacher, this was the time in the school year when things seemed to get louder and at the end of a busy day I'd end up with a headache, trying to calm the noisy storm that the kids were making with the drums and other instruments.

After cleaning up the classroom and taking some work home to mark, I picked up my belongings and locked the classroom. There weren't many of the other members of staff left in the school by the time I left. On the walk home, I checked my phone and saw that my aunt had phoned and left a message and that both James and David had texted. I decided to answer them when I'd got home and changed out of my work clothes.

As I approached my front door, I saw that sitting waiting on the step was a single yellow rose with no note or card. Picking it up, I unlocked my front door in the hope that a note had been put through my letterbox, but there wasn't anything. I rested the rose on the kitchen workbench, put the kettle on, and went to get changed. After making a cup of tea, I phoned Auntie May back. We had a thirty-minute chat and, after some reassurance from me that I was ok after last night's visit, I promised to stop by on Wednesday after school for dinner. Then I phoned James back just to reassure him that all was well. I then went back to work, marking the children's work I'd brought home and making a poster for the community centre to put up for the choir group. With these done and dinner on, I texted David back.

Jane: Thank you for the text this morning. I'm ok. I've spoken to James and Auntie May just to keep them up to date.

David: No problem. Let me know if you need anything. I will see you on Friday, if not before.

Jane: Thank you.

I was still confused about the mystery rose; I thought I would ask him.

Jane: Can I just ask if you put a yellow rose on my doorstep today?"

No sooner had I sent the text than my phone started ringing. It was David.

"Hi Jane. I'm sorry, I don't understand what you meant when you asked if I had put a yellow rose on your doorstep. Was there no note?"

"No, there was no note. It was a bit weird. I wondered if it was from you … so I thought I would just ask if you knew anything. I didn't mean to upset you."

"I'm not upset that you asked me. I'm just concerned because it wasn't me that left you a rose, and I'm worried for you. I'm going to come round and see this rose and make sure you are ok."

The phone went quiet. I didn't know how I felt, but one thing was for certain: I needed to put some salad together because, from the sounds of it, I was going to have company and dinner would need to stretch to two people.

Ten minutes later, I heard a car door shut and knew that David had arrived, so I opened the door before he could knock. No sooner had the door opened than David said, "I am so sorry. I realised on the way round here how bossy I sounded, and I didn't mean that I was worried about you, so if you want me to go home, I will, but I guess I just panicked."

"I was a bit taken a back, especially when I tried to talk to you and tell you I was ok, but you had already put the phone down. I didn't mean for you to drop everything and come round," I said to him as I let him into the house.

"I am sorry again, and I will leave if you want me to. I also think that, while I am being honest and maybe in your bad books, you ought to know I phoned James about the rose, and he and Lacy are on their way over as well."

Laughing at him I said, "You really did panic, didn't you?"

Just as he finished talking, James and Lacy arrived. Lacy was carrying a much-needed bottle of wine. I wouldn't normally drink on a school night, but in all honesty, I was worried about the rose and who it was from. Normally in this village, no one could do anything without everyone knowing. James and David went off to investigate the rose. I didn't know what they expected to learn from it. Lacy and I stood behind them rolling our eyes as they gave the flower a post-mortem.

After putting a dinner on the table of left-over roast chicken, salad, and boiled potatoes, pouring out the wine between us, we all sat down to eat as James started his interrogation. "Why didn't you tell me about the rose when you spoke to me? How did you find it on your doorstep? Was anyone around at the time? Have you had any messages from anyone saying they left you a little present? Do you think it could be Peter?"

At that I laughed. "Are you joking? He never bought me flowers when we were together. What on earth makes you think he would do so now? Peter never does things if won't get anything out of it."

Lacy and James laughed and agreed that the possibility that it had come from Peter was very slim. After dinner, Lacy and I tidied up while the great detectives went through a list of suspects. Honestly, you would think it was something sinister that had been put on my doorstep, not a single rose!

"James, David, can you just stop for a minute? It was just a rose. It wasn't a bomb. Why are you both so upset and concerned about it? What do you know that I don't?"

Both of them looked at me, and James said, "Jane, no one I know would leave a rose on someone's doorstep without a note, and as you know, around here everyone knows everything, so surely someone would have seen something."

We had just finished loading the dishwasher when Lacy asked, "Are you alright?"

"I was when I was on my own, but with the great detectives in there, they are starting to frighten me a bit. I don't think it was anything sinister, and while it would be nice to know who put it there and why, I'm not frightened by it."

Giving me a hug, she replied, "I can understand that. Just ignore them. They will get bored when they realise they can't solve the conundrum."

I always knew that Lacy was special and that she deserved nothing but good to happen to her, especially after everything she had gone through at school. I was so glad we had managed to become great friends recently – in fact, we felt more like sisters, which was good because James and I were so close.

We went into the living room, and Lacy said, "Alright, dynamic duo, we aren't going to solve this mystery tonight. And it's a school night. Jane needs to get ready for tomorrow, and I have a very important meeting tomorrow morning with you, David. So, I suggest we stop for the night. Let's make a group chat so we can text easily, and if there are any developments with the mysterious rose, Jane will keep us updated."

James laughed and said, "I love it when she gets bossy. Ok, I'm coming." He stood up and gave me a kiss on the cheek and a cuddle before saying goodnight to both me and David, who had also stood up.

With a smile on my face, I turned to David, who said, "I'd better go as well ... I'll text you tomorrow. Make sure you lock the door behind me and set your burglar alarm."

"I will, and thank you for coming, David. I hope it didn't inconvenience you too much."

"No problem. Anytime," he replied and planted a kiss on my cheek.

After locking the door behind him, I let out a breath as

I leaned against the door. All I'd wanted was a quiet night in to decompress from school. Instead, although it was nice, I ended up having a dinner party for four.

I set my alarm, turned everything off, and went to bed with my e-reader, but no sooner had I opened my book I fell asleep.

Tuesday, Wednesday, and Thursday went by without any drama. Each day on the group chat as soon as I got home James messaged to ask if I had any other gifts left for me, but there hadn't been anything.

Then on Friday, which was my birthday, I woke up with a text from an unknown number wishing me a happy birthday. I had quick conversation with Auntie May and Uncle Mike and a text from the group chat wishing me a happy birthday, all before I went to work, where there were a few cards and presents from staff and some of the students. The rest of the day went by quite quickly and surprisingly easily, which is unusual for a Friday, but that day was definitely one of the calmest Fridays I'd had in a long time. Locking up and walking home, I was thinking of what I was going to wear tonight to David's restaurant, Fish by The River. When I got to my gate, I realised that there was another rose on my doorstep. Attached to it was a typed note that said, 'Happy Birthday' and nothing more. I picked it up and had a look around - there was no one there. I went inside and turned the alarm off, put the rose in the kitchen, and took a picture of it and the note and sent it to the group chat with the words, "Don't panic, and I don't want to talk about it tonight, but I got another rose - this time with a note."

James: "What the hell. We *need* to talk about it tonight."

Lacy: "James, calm down and let's do what Jane wants and enjoy tonight."

David: "I am with James, but I think we need to enjoy ourselves tonight, so no more mention of this until tomorrow."

James: "Ok, but we are picking you up, Jane. I don't want you coming out on your own."

Deciding that was going to be the best answer I was going to get, I agreed, and we arranged that they would pick me up at 6.30 as we were meeting Auntie May and Uncle Mike at 6.45 in the restaurant bar.

I started to get ready as I didn't have long. At least I had already decided what I was going to wear. Pushing all thoughts of the rose out of my mind, I got all dolled up, ready to face the world, and just as I got my shoes on, James knocked on the door.

We decided that James wouldn't drive to the restaurant

as it wasn't far to walk and it would mean that we could all have a drink. That was one of the many wonderful things about living in the village: nothing was too far away. We arrived at the restaurant ten minutes later.

David

I made sure that the private dining room was all ready for Jane's birthday meal. There was something about her that brought out the protective side of me. I went to the corner shop the other day and heard this woman talking about her. Although it didn't require a great detective to work out, I realised that the person who was talking was Sarah, the woman who had slept with Peter. Her friend told her to shut up, doing my job for me. Jane needed a break from it all, and hopefully tonight would give her that break.

I had just entered the bar when May and Mike came in, so I went over to greet them and noticed that May had bought the promised coffee birthday cake, which was Jane's favourite cake, using the recipe her mum used to make for her. The cake needed to be offloaded before the birthday girl came in. I told them everything was set up in the room and the presents were all on the table.

"Thank you for everything, David. I hope you're going to join us tonight. I know that you and Jane have been getting to know each other, but knowing Jane, she would like you to join us but doesn't want to ask, so I'm going to," May said as she handed me the cake.

Mike added, "There's no point arguing with her, so just agree," and winked at me.

Laughing, I agreed and told them I would be back in a minute whilst I took the cake to the kitchen fridge. I spoke the waiter who was going to work in the dining room, and I prewarned the staff that I would also be eating. I then went back to the bar just as James, Lacy, and Jane walked in.

Jane wore a fitted red dress, which highlighted her perfect curves and matching red heeled shoes, making her tall enough to be nearly towering over May.

Walking over to greet them, I gave Lacy and Jane a kiss on the cheek and shook James' hand. James whispered in my ear, "I hope you are joining us for dinner."

"Of course," I whispered back. "What can I get you to drink?"

With everyone's drink orders placed at the bar, I suggested that we go up to the room and the drinks could follow. With everyone's agreement, Jane and I led the way. I guided her with my hand on her lower back. What struck me as I touched her was a feeling of calm and warmth, and I think she felt it too as she relaxed as we walked.

After opening the door to the party room, Jane stopped short and exclaimed, "Wow!" The room was decked out with flowers and pink birthday balloons. "I really didn't expect this! It's too much. It's not like it's a special birthday."

Walking over to her, May gave her a hug and said, "You deserve it. *You* are special, and you deserve this treat as much as anyone else, so sit down and enjoy yourself. First, though, I think we have time for a few presents. David, could you pass some presents to Jane, please?"

Everyone took a seat, and I went over to the table with the presents on and picked up one to give to Jane. As she took it, she thanked me with a kind smile. Watching her unwrap one of the gifts that James and Lacy had bought her was mesmerising because she was concentrating on opening it so carefully, but I could see the joy on her face before she had even got to the present. She did this for every single present she received, and, unlike my ex-wife, none of her expressions seemed fake and none of her expressions said, "Oh god, what were they thinking? I can't wait to take this back to the shop and exchange it." In fact, there was nothing Jane did that seemed fake. What you see is what you get with Jane, and that was one of the things I liked about her. The couples, May and Mike and James and Lacy, sat next to each other, leaving me to sit next to Jane. I was worried about buying her a present. I didn't know what to buy her and was thinking of just getting her some flowers, but I had been walking past the village shop, where they had a few gift ideas, and as soon as I saw the necklace with a music note on it, I knew it would be perfect for her. As she opened my present to her, she said, "You didn't need to get me anything."

"I know I didn't. But I saw it and thought of you."

I was so relieved that she liked it. I always have anxiety giving people presents because every gift I ever gave Stephanie she'd thrown back in my face. Jane looked so happy when she first saw the necklace, and I am sure I heard her whisper "It's beautiful". As soon as I heard that, I relaxed and started to enjoy the evening more. I didn't realise how worried I had been about my choice.

Dinner was soon served. Jane had picked the stuffed plaice with a shrimp sauce. I had the tuna, and, as usual, the chef did me proud.

After dinner it was time for the cake and traditional singing of Happy Birthday, although we all told James not to sing as he had the voice of the devil. Sitting with Jane and her family was really relaxing, and, in some ways, it made me miss my family, even though it had been six years since mum and dad had died in the accident. I had no family left, but laughing and joking with Jane's family was comforting and made me feel like I belonged there, which was something I had never felt before with another family. The evening was starting to round off at 10.30, and because the restaurant was also closing, there weren't many tables left that needed cleaning. I was just getting ready to say goodbye to everyone when Jane invited me and everyone else back to hers for a drink. May and Mike declined, but James and Lacy agreed as neither of them had to go to work the next day. After checking to see if I was needed in the restaurant, I accepted the invitation. Late nights didn't really affect me due to spending so long working in the restaurant trying to get it up and running.

The four of us set off to Jane's house, carrying her presents. May and Mike took the remainder of the cake back to theirs for the barbeque that week as Jane didn't think she would be able to eat it all on her own.

The walk as usual was full of laughter as the three of us decided to gang up on James and give him a hard time. I started it by teasing him about the time we were in university.

"When James was at uni, he was so unorganised! He used to always cut it fine for class. It was as if he would suddenly remember he needed to be somewhere."

"Oh, come on, I wasn't that bad."

"Yes you were! Do you remember when one of the lectures changed rooms but you didn't know? By the time you realised and had run to the right room, the lecturer was not happy, especially as we had started group work already. When you turned up, your face was bright red and you were doubled over, finding it hard to breathe."

We were laughing at the vision this was giving us as we know James so well so teasing him was fun I had to of course j0oin in, what are cousins for if it's n9ot to embarrass each other. "You haven't improved since school James do you remember you did that in school once. Do you remember? You were told by the teacher, I can't remember what her name was because she was a temp, but she asked if you would be late if you were paid to be there, and you replied, 'Oh, I didn't realise getting paid was an option. I would definitely take that option. It would be silly not to.' She was speechless! But you just stood there with your cheeky grin."

"I remember hearing about that," Lacy added. "I remember one of the teachers even saying, 'That's James for you'. I'm glad things have changed and you have grown up. Or have you?" She laughed.

"Oh, come on, Lacy. that's not fair. I have grown up, well, most of the time anyway."

It was nice to see Jane and Lacy relaxed and enjoying themselves. They had both been through so much, and it showed how strong the women were. James also seemed more laid back and settled than I had ever seen him.

We got to Jane's house, and suddenly, she stopped, and her face went white as she saw on her doorstep a present wrapped up in a yellow ribbon. As soon as James saw the present, I could see the steam coming out of his ears, but I knew that my response was just the same. As with the roses, there was no note. James picked up the present, and we went inside Jane's house, by which time Jane was shaking. Lacy set about making everyone a coffee while I sat on the sofa with Jane, trying to calm her down, while James looked in the box. I looked over towards him as he pulled out a small soft teddy wearing a plain white t-shirt with a yellow rose on the front.

"Who keeps putting things on my doorstep? Why are they doing this to me?" Jane asked.

"I don't know, but we are going to find out. James and I are going to put a camera in your doorbell. That way, we can record whoever it is leaving these gifts," I replied, then I asked Lacy if she would sit with Jane while I had a chat with James.

Having found James, and with the pretence that we were going to look outside, I said to him, "I'm worried about her. These gifts are beginning to get to her, and I don't care if she says she's fine. She isn't."

"I'm glad that you don't buy Jane's go-to words when she doesn't want to worry people. I feel the same, and I'm glad that you are interested in her. You both deserve to be happy," he replied.

"I didn't tell you that I was interested in her, but I'm glad you approve. There is something about Jane that I can't let go of. She does deserve to be happy, but with the things that Peter did, she needs to be herself and to know who that is, and while these roses are still being left for her, I'm worried that she is going to go back into her shell."

"I'm worried that she is going to fall apart if we leave her on her own. I know this is a big ask, and I wouldn't normally ask this, but is there any chance that you can stay until she is ok?"

"No problem. I will stay as long as she wants me here. Did I hear you say that you were going into town tomorrow? If you are, can you buy one of those small CCTV camera doorbells so that we can put it up and see if we can catch this person?" I replied.

"That's a good idea! Why haven't we thought about that before? I think we should also tell mum and dad; I know they won't be able to do anything, but they would be even more worried about them if the village gossip gets to them first," he said as we walked back inside to see the girls.

Jane

I really don't know who is doing this, but it is starting to frighten me. It was ok when it was just one rose, because then I could kid myself that it was a mistake - someone putting it on the wrong doorstep or the wind blowing it in. But not now.

James and David came into the living room, and the moment I knew was coming happened as James told me that he and Lacy had to go. As soon as I heard those words, I started to panic. I really didn't want to be left on my own, but I couldn't ask them to stay. The next thing I knew was David sitting next to me and holding my hand and asking me if "It was ok", but I think I must have been in panic mode because I didn't know what he was talking about. In the end, I had to ask him what he meant.

"James and Lacy have to go, but is it ok if I stay for a little while?" he asked.

"Oh, sorry, yes, that would be lovely," I said, trying to smile, but I didn't even have it in me to make it convincing. Suddenly aware that I hadn't offered anyone a cup of tea, I leapt out of my seat and asked everyone if they wanted a drink.

I felt myself being turned around to face David. "Honey, Lacy made us all a drink. Sit down here and I will pass it to you now," David said as he helped me sit back down then passed me my tea.

"Oh yes, I'm sorry," I replied.

"Are you sure you are going to be ok if Lacy and I leave? You could always stay at ours for the night. I'm not sure I want to leave you on your own like this," James said.

'Sorry, I just don't understand what is going on … but I will be fine. Don't you worry. David is going to stay. I don't want whoever is doing this to win by driving me out of my home. It will be fine, I promise." I didn't know who I was trying to convince, but after looking at James, he nodded as if acknowledging that things would be ok. He and Lacy got up to leave but not before making sure I knew that I could ring them at any time.

"Jane, I hope you realise that I'm not just staying for a couple of minutes. I'm staying here all night. I don't want to leave you on your own, and I know that if I did leave, I would just worry about you," David said whilst holding my hand.

"Thank you, I appreciate that. I don't mean to be an inconvenience, but these little gifts are really starting to worry me. I can put some fresh sheets on the spare bed for you. Although it's not the best bed, it would be more comfortable than the sofa. I have spare toiletries in the bathroom cabinet, and I bought some men's toiletries sets in the Christmas sale last year for the school fair that you could use. Is it ok if I go to bed? You are more than welcome to watch TV, just make yourself at home. But I am exhausted."

"No problem, and stop apologising. None of this is your fault. I'm going to bed as well, but first I will check that everything is locked up down here."

Leaving David downstairs to make sure everything was secure, I went to my room, and although I didn't think I would, I fell fast asleep in minutes.

"Why are you doing this? Leave me alone! Get off me!" I was screaming. Was it in my dream or out loud? But through the fog I could hear a voice I recognised call me.

"Jane, come, on wake up. You're just having a bad dream. Come on, wake up, it's me, David."

I was beginning to understand what was happening, and as I woke up, I could feel tears on my cheek. "Oh, David, I am so sorry, I don't know what happened."

"It's ok, honey, it was just a bad dream. I'm going to get you a glass of water, but I will be right back."

I didn't want to be left on my own. Things were getting out of hand, and I was scared. Whether it was due to the events leading up to today or the nightmare, I didn't know, but I didn't want to be left alone. I needed to ask David to sleep in the bed with me. My stomach clenched at the idea; my body started to shake, but I was trying so hard to control it that I think I was making it worse. The palms of my hands were sweaty as questions ran around my head. What would he think? Would it scare him off? I hated looking so vulnerable. I needed to get myself together. I was a strong person, and he was a great guy, but I wasn't sure that I was in the right headspace to jump into another relationship, and I wasn't sure that David saw me like that either. This had just got so complicated.

David came back into my room carrying a glass of water. It was only at that moment that I realised he was only wearing his boxer shorts, and I couldn't help looking at that chest. Talk about a six pack! I had never seen anything like it before, and I wondered if my eyes would ever see anything so spectacular again. I don't think David understood because he apologised for only wearing his boxer shorts. He'd heard me screaming and come running without thinking. To lighten up the worry that I could feel coming from David, I decided now was the time to try to make him laugh.

"Oh, there's no need to apologise to me. I can't think of a better sight to calm me when I have just woken up from a nightmare." I gave him a cheeky smile.

He sat on the bed and passed me the glass of water he was

carrying. "Ha ha, glad to be of some assistance. Now, are you ok? Is there anything you need?" David's face showed nothing but concern.

I needed to be brave and ask him to stay. I really didn't think I would be able to go back to sleep on my own.

"I hope it's ok to ask this, but would it be ok if you stayed in here with me? I don't think I can go back to sleep on my own. I understand if you don't want to …"

Before I could finish what I was going to say, David put his finger across my lips and said, "Ssshhh. I can't think of anywhere I would rather be. Now let me into the bed, put your glass down, and let's try to get some sleep, ok?"

"Thank you, yes." As soon as David got under the covers, I felt much better. I felt protected and as if nothing else could hurt me, and those feelings only deepened when he pulled me towards him so that he could hold me. This position must have worked its magic because the next thing I knew it was morning and I was lying in my bed on my own.

Having got out of bed, I went to the bathroom and found David in the living room talking on his phone. Giving him a smile, I went to the kitchen to make a cup of coffee, and a couple of minutes later he followed me and put his arms around me. "Are you feeling better this morning?" he asked.

"Yes, thank you. I really appreciate what you did for me last night. I didn't mean to fall apart like that. Do you want a coffee?"

"Yes, please. And I do wish you would stop apologising! Your reaction was normal. We will find out who is doing this and why. I promise you that. Now, what do you have planned today? I have spoken to Rebecca at the restaurant, and I am free for the next couple of days. I want to spend them with you if that's ok?"

I couldn't think of anything better, but I didn't really have much planned for today other than Auntie May's barbeque. But if it meant I got to spend the day with David, I would do anything. Having gone through my plans for today, which included the exciting washing and hoovering, we decided he would go back to his house for the morning while I got on with the mundane chores and then, at lunch time, we would have a nice lunch out. After finishing our coffee and toast, David loaded the dishwasher and then left to go back to his house, probably to do the same thing I had to do. Clothes don't wash themselves, so I put the washer on and started the other chores. Just as I had unplugged the hoover, the doorbell rung, and David was back.

We decided to go to the pub for lunch because it wasn't great weather. It was drizzling one moment, then the sun was shining, then it started drizzling again. It was as if the weather couldn't really decide what mood it was in.

Walking into the pub, we were met by many of the people I went to school with, and of course mum's and Auntie May's friend, Lily. Wrapping her arms around me, Lily said, "Happy Birthday for yesterday. I was planning on bringing your present to May's barbeque because I wasn't sure when I would see you."

"Thank you, Lily, but I tell you every year that you don't need to buy me anything."

"Of course I do, you are my goddaughter after all."

"Thank you."

There was a table that seated twelve people, and sitting there were some of the local people, including Lily and Mrs Baker. From what I understood, a couple of them had come in that morning when the pub opened and then the group had just got bigger from there; some had meals and some had just come in for a drink. We joined them, and I introduced David to everyone because I wasn't sure who he knew and who he didn't. David and I decided to share a steak sandwich as we knew we were going to get lots of food at Auntie May's tonight.

The food was delicious as always, and it was nice seeing everyone, but the time flew past, and before we knew it, it was three o'clock, and I had promised Auntie May I would help set things up. David drove us there because we were still unsure about the weather, and, on the way there, he told me that James and he had discussed telling Auntie May about the gifts. Whilst I didn't want to worry her, I also didn't want her to find out from someone else. I knew that James and Lacy were going to be helping at the barbeque as well, so I suggested we told both May and Mike before we started setting up because I knew that if we put it off, it would never happen.

Letting ourselves in as usual, I heard Lacy and James talking to my aunt and uncle. When we walked into the living room, Uncle Mike stood up and walked towards me, giving me a kiss on the cheek, and shook David's hand.

"How is my favourite niece this afternoon?" he asked.

"Uncle, I am your *only* niece, but I am ok. There's something I need to tell you both before we do anything," I replied.

Everyone sat down, with me and David on the sofa. I grabbed his hand in the hopes that it would ground me. "Before I start, I want you to know that I am ok and there is nothing to worry about, but I thought you needed to know. A couple of weeks ago, strange things started happening. Someone kept leaving one yellow rose on my doorstep with no note, and none of my neighbours had seen anything. Another rose was left yesterday while I was at work. Then, last night, while I was out for dinner, a box with a small teddy bear was left on the doorstep, and, like the others, there was no note saying who it was from. David and James have been wonderful at trying to reassure me that things will be ok, and David stayed last night. In all honesty, last night's gift frightened me more than anything. James and David said that they are going to get some kind of doorbell with a camera in it in the hopes that we can catch whoever is doing it, and hopefully we'll find out that it's just a silly prank."

Uncle Mike and Auntie May looked at each other. Mike then said, "Are you sure you are all right? Have you spoken to Connor about this? Are they keeping an eye on you?"

David asked, "Just to check, Connor is the policeman that has just been promoted in the village, but you all went to school with him?"

My uncle responded, "Yes he is. He's a lovely lad, would do anything for anyone. He really is an asset to the village."

Trying to get the whole conversation over with because I didn't want them to worry about me, I said, "I'm fine, really. I know James spoke to Connor the other night, but there isn't much the police can do. But every time something is put on my doorstep, James texts Connor, so at least they are aware. Everything will be ok. I don't want you to worry, but I didn't want anyone else to tell you, because you know what living here is like. The place thrives on gossip! So shall we get set up for tonight's barbeque?"

"Ok, as long as you are sure," Auntie May said. "We have decided that in light of the weather, we are just going to use the gazabo for the food and move all the furniture back against the wall in all the downstairs rooms so that people can be in the dry. So, if the men do the setting up in here, Lacy, Jane, and I can start on the food preparation." As with everything Auntie May said, we all fell in line with her orders.

People started to arrive from around five o'clock. After all the setting up, the moment I had just sat down for the first time since we had arrived, David came up to me, put his arm around me, and asked, "Are you alright? Can I get you anything to drink?" Smiling up at him, I told him I was ok and asked if he wanted to join me. He sat next to me, and we watched everyone laughing and joking. To be honest, I was feeling a bit out of sorts, tired after last night's nightmare. I wanted to have an early night tonight. Having talked to Auntie May, we decided that we were going to leave shortly.

After helping Auntie May put her downstairs rooms back the way they were, David and I left to go back to my house. I was surprised when we got to my doorstep. It was empty, and there were no more gifts.

David

I had a lovely relaxing day for the first time in a while. Although I was tired, I didn't want the evening to end. Just by being close to Jane I could feel the tension coursing through her. As we got nearer to her house, I asked if she was ok, and I barely heard her reply of, "Yes, I'm fine." Drawing up outside her house, she looked over towards the door, as I had, and we both saw that the doorstep was empty. Having acknowledged that, she relaxed, smiled at me, and asked me in for a drink.

As I was watching her in the kitchen making our drinks, she turned and smiled one of her heart-stoppings smiles. I had to kiss her. I walked towards her and, cupping her jaw, I lowered my head. Jane rose on her toes, closing the distance between us faster. I tried to show some restraint while I kissed her as I watched her eyes flutter closed. To start with, it was just our lips that were involved, but I started to tease her to see how far I could take this kiss, and I ran my tongue along her bottom lip. My hand gently held the back of her head so I could easily hold her in place, but there was still enough give if Jane decided she wanted to put a stop to it at any point. As far as I was concerned, the house would have to have been on fire before I could put a stop to this kiss, especially as her arms snaked around my neck. In the end, it wasn't a fire that put a stop to the kiss, it was the constant ringing of a phone, and as soon as we came up for breath, we realised that it was her mobile, and from the personalised ringtone, it seemed James was ringing. Jane answered it, but as soon as I looked over to her, I saw the blood drain from her face.

I thought she was going to fall down, so I walked towards her, and I heard her say, "I am on my way." She put the phone down and just stared at it, then her back straightened. She took a deep breath and said out loud, "Right, think, Jane. You need your bag and car keys. Come on, you can do it."

"Jane," I said, but there was no response. I didn't know what the phone call was about, but she was in her own little world. "Jane," I repeated, but this time I stood in front of her so that she would notice me.

"I can't stop, I need to go," she replied.

"Jane, calm down, you can't go anywhere in this state. Take a deep breath in, then out. Come on, breathe with me, that's right. Now, can you tell me what is happening? Is James alright?"

"James is ok, but Uncle Mike has been rushed to the hospital with a suspected heart attack. I need to go."

"Jane, you have just had a panic attack and you are in shock. I'll drive you to the hospital. Take a deep breath and then we can go. But first, come here."

Opening my arms, she walked into them. I gave her a

cuddle, but I wouldn't let her go until I was sure she had calmed down enough to think straight. After a couple of minutes, she had calmed down enough for us to leave for the hospital.

Luckily, it didn't take us long to get to the hospital as the traffic was light. Walking into the accident and emergency department, there was no one waiting at the desk, so I went over to ask the receptionist where we could find May and James. They directed us to a little room just off the main waiting area.

The door opened, and the first thing we saw was a row of connected plastic chairs on both sides of the room. The walls were mainly plain white, except for one picture with a flower on it. Tucked away in the corner was a water cooler with small plastic cups and sitting on top of that was a box of tissues. James and Lacy were sitting together on one side, and May was sitting opposite them. The room was narrow enough to allow James to hold his mum's hand while he was sitting on the edge of the seat on the opposite side of the room. When we opened the door, they looked up.

On spotting May, Jane ran over and sat next to her. It was the first time I had seen May the strongest woman I have ever known crumble. I walked over to James, who had hold of Lacy as if his life depended on it. Squeezing James' shoulder to let him know that I was there and giving Lacy a reassuring smile, I went back to where Jane sat trying to reassure and calm her aunt. I grabbed Jane's free hand.

May suddenly looked up, and while wiping her tears away from her face, she said, "Oh, David, I'm sorry, I didn't see you arrive. I must look a state."

Reassuring her, I said, "Don't be silly, May, you look magnificent as always." She tried to smile, but I could see the worry on her face.

We had been sitting there for around ten minutes when the door opened and the doctor came in. May stood up quicker than any of us anticipated. James stood up and went to hold on to his mum while the doctor spoke to them. The doctor said, "Mike is in a stable condition. As the paramedics thought, he had a heart attack and is being moved to the acute cardiac care ward shortly, where they will treat him for a non-ST-elevation myocardial infarction. He was lucky as this was not as severe as it could have been and meant that the blood was only partially blocked, therefore a smaller section of the heart was affected, and alongside monitoring, it is easily treated with blood thinning medication, which he will need to stay on until he has an outpatient's appointment to see the heart specialist. We want to keep him in the hospital at least for tonight just to keep an eye on him as his body has gone into shock. As soon as he is moved to the ward, you can visit him, but if you have any questions, please don't hesitate to ask."

"Thank you, doctor, we really appreciate everything you have done." And with that, the doctor left. James got May back in the chair.

"That's good, isn't it?, it's better than we expected and it has been a shock for all of us, but we will be able to see him shortly and you can tell him off for scaring us" James said to his mum.

"It is, thank heavens."

As soon as Mike was moved into the ward, May and James went to see him, but as soon as they left, Jane just crumbled. Luckily, Lacy could see what was happening and managed to grab Jane before she fell to her knees. Together, we managed to get her to the nearest chair, but I don't think she really knew what was going on. Lacy found a packet of tissues in her bag and got her some water while I tried to calm her down.

It took a good twenty minutes before Jane's crying turned into hiccups. We managed to get her to drink some water, and just as she was calming down, the door opened and James walked in. His face and body were less tense than they were when he'd left. Knowing James as I do, I know that he was holding his feelings inside for the benefit of his mum and Jane. Only when he got home would James let his feelings out, and Lacy would have to have to help him through this. Walking over to Jane, he bent down so that he was the same height to look her in the eye. Taking her hand, he said to her, "Jane, look at me. He's alright, it was just a bit of a shock for everyone. He's asking for you, but first I want you to go with Lacy and wash your face. Otherwise, Mum will take one look at you and start crying herself, and believe it or not, Dad is trying to keep her calm."

Lacy stood up and took Jane's hand to take her to the nearest toilet to clean her face and try and cover up some of the evidence that she was upset.

Meanwhile, James sat down next to me with a huge breath, his head in his hands, and said to me, "Thanks for being here, it really means a lot. I never want to get that phone call from Mum ever again. I'm just glad I have Lacy because I kind of lost it there for a while."

"Don't be silly. You know I love your family. They have done so much for me. How is your dad really?"

"He's taking most of it quite well, although knowing Dad, it's going to take a lot of persuading for him to understand what he can and can't do. I'm just glad he's sitting up and trying to cheer Mum up, although I didn't see him before he was blue-lighted here. Mum said she thought he was dead as he wasn't responding and was grey. I am so glad we were near the hospital because we beat Mum here. I don't think she would have coped if she was all alone waiting for us."

Lacy and Jane returned. Although her eyes were still visibly puffy, that was the only evidence of her breakdown.

James took her hand and smiled at her. "Now, remember, it's up for a smile and not down for a frown." She laughed and left with James to go and see Mike, leaving Lacy and me waiting for them to return.

Making sure Lacy was ok to be left on her own, I went off to get everyone hot drinks. I knew that May needed something. In the time we had been there she hadn't even had so much as a drink of water, and trying to persuade her to leave the hospital was going to be difficult. The last thing anyone needed was for May to make herself ill by not eating and drinking due to her worrying and putting everyone else's needs first.

I had only been back a couple of minutes when the three of them returned. After distributing the much-needed drinks, Jane and James set about on the difficult task of trying to persuade May that she shouldn't be on her own tonight. After a lot of arguing, James and Lacy insisted that they stay with her as the hospital thought that Mike would only be kept in for 24 hours. Eventually, May agreed. If everything went to plan, and Mike was discharged tomorrow, James would collect him while Lacy stayed with May and Jane would pop in after school finished for the day.

Having finished her drink, May went back to say goodnight to Mike. She hadn't been long before she came back and told Lacy and me that Mike wanted to see us.

Entering the room, Mike looked up and said to us both, "Are you two doing alright?" I looked at Lacy, who appeared as confused by the question as I was.

"Erm, Mike, we are supposed to ask you that question, not the other way around," I replied.

"That's true. You're probably wondering why I wanted to see the two of you, and it isn't to reveal who the murderer is."

We all laughed at his week attempt at a joke. At least he still had his odd sense of humour.

"Well, yeah, we are wondering," Lacy replied as she sat on the chair next to Mike's bed.

"I need you to both promise me that you will keep an eye on your significant others, and, before you deny it, David, we all know that Jane is your significant other. We all know that you both have feelings for each other. The damage Peter caused with Jane's trust means that it's going to take a while for her to trust fully, however, you will get there, but I am worried that she could take this illness hard. She won't be the only one, but

I will handle May when I am out of here as well, as I normally do, and I will put up with as much mothering as that woman can inflict on me, because I would be nothing without her.

"I promise to look after her," I said. Mike's words made me realise how worried Jane's family had been when she was with Peter and how powerless that had made them feel.

"I know that Jane will put all her energy into trying to help me, May, and James and ignore what she needs. She's just beginning to show more of herself after the Peter debacle. I have never liked him as I could see over time that he was trying to quash her for his own goals, ignoring what she needs. We tried to help as much as she would let us, but we always made it clear that we were there for her and we loved her unconditionally. She needs someone better, someone who can see the real Jane, and we think you are that man. She is going to need you to help her get over the shock of what just happened to me. Right now, she is going to be remembering her mother and the various hospital visits she had to make while her mum was dying."

"As for you, Lacy, you know what James is like. You have known him a long time. You need to break down the brick wall that he is currently building before it gets too big. He will say he's ok on the outside, but you can see through that. Now, both of you go and get out of here and let an old man sleep."

"I am a great bulldozer these days, Mike," Lacy replied.

"As if you're an old man, Mike! We are going to leave you now because you need to have a nice sleep, and we will see you tomorrow," I replied.

Leaning over, Lacy gave him a kiss on the cheek, but I could see tears in her eyes, which would have seen echoed in my eyes if she had looked back at me. She had just managed to turn away from the bed when Mike called her again.

"Oh, Lacy, before you go, I just wanted to say I really appreciate you staying with May tonight. It will take her mind off worrying about me, and I will see you both tomorrow when I'm not wearing a hospital gown."

With that, we left Mike's room, and both of us seemed lost in our own heads as Mike's words were rang through our minds. We both knew James and Jane so well, and everything he said was true. Breaking the silence on the way back to the waiting room, Lacy touched my arm to stop me walking.

"David, I just want you to know that James and I agree with everything Mike said in there. You are the best thing to happen to Jane in a long time, but take it from someone who knows, it's going to take time to get through the defences she has put up to protect herself. But as I am sure you know, she is worth it, as are you. We just need to get through the next few days and figure out who it is leaving flowers on her doorstep."

"Thank you, that means a lot. We just need Jane to realise that I am here for her to rely on and it's ok to be herself and vulnerable with me and that I am not going to turn my back on her. Now, come on, let's get back to them and do what Mike said."

We went back to the waiting room, where everyone was ready to leave. James and Lacy took May home, and I took a sombre Jane home. I could tell that her mind was a hundred miles away and she was putting her defence mechanism in place.

As I pulled up to her place, she turned around and said to me, "I really appreciate everything you have done for me today. I don't know how to thank you."

Just as I was about to reply, she screamed, "What the hell!" As I was looking at her, I saw the colour drain from her face as I followed where she was looking. Not just one rose was sitting on her doorstep. There were scattered rose petals covering her front step and a rose laid on the top.

'Stay in the car until I check things out,' I said to her, and then I got out and locked the car doors with her sitting frozen in the passenger seat. I went round the whole house to see if the roses were just in that place and whether or not there was anything else amiss.

Having checked around the house and found nothing, I went to get Jane out of the car only to find tears streaming down her face. But she wasn't making a noise. She was frozen in time.

Walking over to her door, which I had already unlocked, I said, "Come on, darling, let's get you inside." I put my hand out to help her out of the car. I hoped my face showed a reassuring smile. I certainly didn't want to show how angry I was that someone was trying to frighten her. She walked inside her house like a robot, following her normal actions of putting her keys in the bowl by her door, taking her coat off, and hanging it up. I could tell just by looking at her face, which was devoid of all emotion, that she had shut down. Maybe it was because of the last few hours with her uncle's illness or maybe it was due to the stress of the roses being put on her doorstep. Whatever it was, I never wanted to see that look on her face again.

"I am going to put the kettle on and make you a cup of tea, but first I want to clear that mess up out the front. Why don't you sit on the sofa? I will be right back," I told her and helped her onto the sofa. Then I went into the kitchen and flicked the switch on the kettle before getting the dustpan and brush to clear up outside. But before cleaning up, I first took a picture so that I could show James and Connor. Having cleaned up the mess and thrown it in her compost bin, I walked past the sitting room towards the kitchen and noticed that she hadn't moved from the position she was in when I'd left her. In fact, she looked like a statue.

Having made the tea and taken it into the sitting room, I saw that although she still hadn't moved. She was sitting there quietly crying. I put the mugs down on her coffee table and sat next to her, pulling her close so that she was leaning on me in the hopes that she wouldn't feel so alone.

"Come on, darling, let it all out. You have had an emotional evening. You need to let go, and I am here to catch you," I quietly whispered to her. Just then, the floodgates opened. Like many men, I don't like seeing a woman cry, but she needed to let it out, and I wouldn't leave until I knew that she was calm enough to be left on her own. Jane was such a strong woman, but at that moment she needed support. The last few weeks of getting to know Jane had shown me that, although she was strong, she'd hide her feelings and didn't think her feelings were important. Well, she was wrong.

After a little while, her crying had slowed down, but then I heard her quietly say, "He can't die, he's like a dad to me."

"Ssshh. It will be ok as long as he does what the doctors have told him to do, and I am sure that May will make sure he does. There are a lot of years left in Mike. It was just his body warning him to take things easy."

"I know you're right; I just can't cope with anything being wrong with him. He has always been there for me. He has always known what to say and when to say it. Oh, Auntie May, how is she going to cope? I'm so selfish I didn't even think of her." She started crying again.

"Jane, look at me." She tentatively turned her head. "You're not selfish. You were great in the waiting room, comforting her and making sure she had everything she needed while Lacy concentrated on calming down James. This has been a shock for everyone, and just because you're now home and thinking about yourself and your feelings, doesn't mean you are selfish. It means you are human. Now dry your eyes and drink your tea. I know it's late, but I'm going to put some mindless TV on so that we can relax in front of it without thinking about anything else, okay?" She gave a little nod, dried her tears with the tissue I had given her, and drank her cold tea.

While I found something on the television that we could sit and watch without concentrating on, Jane went to the bathroom to wash her face, and by the time she had come back, I had found an old black and white film. Lifting my arm up so that Jane could lean on me to watch the TV, she became more comfortable. Her position slowly changed so that by the time the film had finished, her head was resting on my lap and she was fast asleep. I hadn't even noticed that I had been playing with her hair. I had never really been that bothered about playing with a woman's hair before, but there was clearly something calming about it - not just for her, but for me as well.

As soon as the film credits had rolled, I turned the TV off, but I didn't want to wake Jane up if I could help it, so I carefully lifted the pillow up so that her head was resting on it enough for me to be able to get off the sofa and whispered all the time to her, telling her what I was doing in the hopes that she wouldn't wake up in a fright.

"I'm just going to lift you up and carry you into your bedroom. You stay asleep, everything will be alright." Although she moved and roused a little bit, she mostly stayed asleep. It was easy carrying her up the stairs because she didn't seem to weigh much, although from what I had learnt from James, she had put on some weight since splitting up with Peter. Apparently, he had kept on at her about her weight. Putting her on the bed, I was just about to cover her with the covers when I heard her quietly say, "Please stay."

It wasn't as if I was going to leave her. I had planned on staying anyway in case she woke up with another nightmare, but at least now I had her permission, so having made sure she was still asleep, I grabbed a fleece blanket that I saw sitting on the chair in her bedroom and went back into the living room to make myself a bed on the sofa using the cushions that were already on there as pillows. I know I could have used the spare room, but we hadn't discussed me staying and I didn't want to overstep the mark. I took my trousers and shirt off because I knew I wasn't going to be comfortable in them and tried to get to sleep in my t-shirt and boxers. Surprisingly, I fell asleep quite quickly.

Chapter 6

Jane

I woke up a bit confused. I didn't remember going to bed, and I was still wearing the clothes I'd had on the day before. I checked the time on the clock. It was only six o'clock, so I had plenty of time before I needed to leave to go to work. It was only when I was in the shower and my brain had obviously come back online that I remembered falling asleep in front of the television after being at the hospital. I remembered David being here. Just as I finished up in the shower, I remembered asking him to stay. I quickly jumped out of the shower and got dressed into my trousers and blouse, ready for work. I walked quietly and checked the spare bedroom, but there was no one in there. Then I heard faint snoring coming from the living room. Creeping to the doorway, I saw a fast asleep, nearly six-foot tall David on my sofa. *He must be so uncomfortable*, I worried. I didn't want to wake him up, so I quietly went into the kitchen and closed the door to muffle the sound of the boiling kettle.

Having made the coffee and carrying the mugs, I went into the living room to see David waking up.

"Morning, I made you a coffee. I appreciate you staying

here last night, but you didn't need to squeeze onto the sofa. There is a spare room you could have used."

"Morning. It was no problem. I didn't want to go poking around your house when you were asleep, so I thought here would be best, although I think I may need to see a chiropractor." He winced as he stretched his back.

"You're welcome to send me the bill. Thanks again, I really appreciate everything you did for me last night."

"Don't thank me. I'm glad I was here for you."

She smiled. "What do you have planned for the rest of the day?"

"I have to go to the restaurant today. I have some interviews to do for some waiting staff, but I won't be working late, so I should be finished by six o'clock. Are you still going to visit May and Mike after work?"

"Unless I hear differently, I was going to go to theirs, but I wondered if you wanted to come round here for dinner? I was thinking of getting an Indian takeaway, and it's much better shared."

"I would love that, as long as you're sure. Although I have a suggestion … why don't you ring me when you get back from Mike and May's and I will bring the Indian with me? That way, you don't have to worry about getting back for a set time."

"That would be great. Do you want any breakfast? I haven't got much in the house, but I could make you some scrambled eggs on toast or something?"

"Just some toast would be great, if that's ok."

"No problem, it's the least I can do. There's a new toothbrush in the bathroom cabinet and some small bottles of shower gel in there as well if you wanted a shower. I'm not sure you want to spend the day smelling of freesias."

"You're right. All day I'll be smelling of you and thinking you're in the room and I'll be disappointed that you aren't there," he said, laughing.

I smiled. "I will leave you to finish getting up." I really didn't know what else I should say.

I retreated back to the kitchen, hoping that my face wasn't bright red. Although he did appear to have a t-shirt on and I couldn't see much, there was nothing wrong with my imagination, and what I was imagining was out of this world. Taking my mind off things, I managed to put the clean dishes away and put some toast on, and just as it was popping up, David returned fully dressed.

"I was just bringing it through to the living room."

"Let me help."

We sat eating our toast and talked some more about the day ahead.

As he spread honey on his toast, David said, "I have to do four interviews for vacancy today, but I might take on two people as now that the business is up and running, I am trying to cut down on my hours. But I also want Rebecca to do less hours as well. What have you got planned today?"

"I mainly have planning to do today. I have a few classes as well. I need to finish the planning for the school concert and getting the choir up and running. As soon as Peter left, I thought I wanted to restart my singing gigs but I am apprehensive because I have started to realise that I've been changing too much all at one time if you take into account that I have decorated my house the way I want it and that I am restarting the choir along with work I want to have time to be me and discover who I am because of that maybe I need to take things a bit slower."

"I think that's a good idea. I understand you trying to do everything you feel you missed out on, but you need to remember that your health is important, so it might be wise to not rush into too many things."

"Thank you. I am beginning to understand that about myself now. Anyway, I could sit and talk with you all day, but we both need to go."

I carried the plates and mugs to the kitchen and put them in the dishwasher to deal with later. Just as I was turning round, I felt David's hands around my waist, which guided me so that I was in front of him. Looking up, I saw his head bend down towards mine, and he kissed me. It was the second most wonderful kiss I have ever had. The first was when he'd kissed me the day before.

"Wow," I said as soon as we both came up for breath.

"Wow indeed," he said as he rested his head on mine. "Come on, we'd better get on with the day ahead, otherwise we will never move." Much as I wanted to disagree with him, I knew he was right.

David dropped me off at school in his car, giving me a quick kiss before he left to go to his interviews. I went into the staffroom. When I was at school, the staffroom had always been one of those forbidden places that we were never allowed in. I would never forget my first day of walking into the staff room as a teacher. The walls were mainly painted with magnolia, a large pin board with timetables and notes hanging up, and on the other big wall was a huge unit of pigeonholes with all the teachers' names on it. There were a couple of round tables and chairs for anyone who wanted to work, but sitting in the middle of the room was a large u-shaped seating area. Saying hello to all the other teachers who were lining up to get their morning coffee, I walked over to where my fellow teacher and friend, Samantha, or Sam to her friends, was waiting for me with a cup of coffee. Sam was an amazing woman. She always floated through life with a smile on her face. Whether it was because of the smile or because of the fact that she was always wearing flowing dresses and didn't take herself to seriously, people often underestimated her as they thought she could be pushed around. But Sam would fight for those she loved, and there were times when I wouldn't have been able to cope without her.

"Firstly, how is Mike, and does May need anything?"

"They're hoping he can come home today, and as long as he does what he is told, then he should just need monitoring."

"Good. And secondly, do you want to fill me in on why I have just seen you kissing the new boy in the village?"

"Joys of village life." I rolled my eyes. "The new boy? Really? David has lived here nearly two years, and I'm not sure he can be classed as a 'boy'."

"True. From what I could see, he was definitely a man, which is more than can be said for your ex. So come on then, spill! And don't change the subject. I know your little games."

"It's still early days, and we are taking it slow, especially after Peter, but there's something special about him. He's hard working, loyal, and a gentleman. Last night, he stayed the night at my house because I was upset when we left the hospital. I asked him to stay, but by that time I was pretty out of it, and instead of sleeping in the spare room, he slept on the sofa because he didn't want to go around snooping while I was asleep."

"Does he have a brother?" She gave me a cheeky grin. "Only joking. You deserve to be treated like you are special, because you are! And I'm glad he's taking things at your own speed and not pushing you. It's nice to see you smile again. It has been a long time coming."

Just as I was about to answer her, the head teacher came in for our Monday morning meeting. All the staff took their seats ready for the meeting.

"Right, let's start." The head went through who was on playground duty, any visitors we were having in the school this week, and any other special plans for the week ahead. When the meeting finished, there were a few minutes left before the bell rang, and the head called me over.

"Jane, how is Mike? Are you going to be alright working today? I know Mike is like a father to you, and I would understand if you needed a personal day."

"Thank you, he is ok. They are hoping he can come home this afternoon. I really appreciate it, but I will be fine. I'll be going round to see them after school. James and Lacy stayed with May last night so she wouldn't be alone. James will go get him this afternoon. I will let you know if anything changes."

"That's wonderful. Well, as long as you are sure, but please keep me updated."

"I will, thank you."

Luckily, the school day went by really quickly. I had received a message from James at two o'clock saying that he was off to the hospital to collect his dad and that everything was ok and that he would see me later. I knew he didn't expect a reply as he knew phones weren't allowed in school. The classes I taught during the day were quite subdued. Their parents had probably told the kids to be well-behaved today for me. There were a lot of positives to living in a small village; one being that everyone knew what was going on in your life, although that could be a negative as well. Today, it definitely helped.

As soon as the school bell rang, signalling the end of the day, I tidied up the classroom and checked that there was nothing else I needed to do before I went to see my aunt and uncle.

It didn't normally take long to walk from the school to my aunt and uncle's house, but there were so many people coming up to me, checking on how my uncle was, and so many offers of help from people that by the time I got to their house, it was forty-five minutes later. As usual, the front door was unlocked, and, walking in, I heard May and Mike.

'Stop fussing, woman, I am alright. Sit down before you overdo it.'

"I am not fussing; I am just making sure that you are comfortable."

James came out of the kitchen and said to me, "Don't mind them. They have been having the same conversation for ten minutes. I retreated into the kitchen because I am a coward and I couldn't calm mum down, so I left them in the guise of making a cup of tea."

"I don't blame you. I'd better go in there and see if I can do anything to calm her down. But if you're offering, I will have a tea."

"Good luck. I will bring it in shortly. Lacy has just gone to get some milk, so it shouldn't be too long."

"I think she might be a little while. It took me forty-five minutes to walk from the school! So many people stopped me to ask how Mike and May are and if they need any help."

"Don't you just love small village life? Oh, while I remember, I popped in and saw David on the way to pick dad up, and I gave him the camera bell we bought. I think he's planning on fitting it tonight. He also told me about your gift last night."

"I forgot about the new doorbell. I just hope we find out who it is soon."

"We will, don't worry. Now get in there and try to work your magic."

Laughing at the idea that I had enough magic to stop my aunt from fussing over my uncle, I went into the living room.

"Here's my gorgeous girl," my uncle said.

"You look much better than yesterday. How are you?" I asked.

"Don't *you* start fussing. It's bad enough your aunt doing it without you starting as well."

"I wouldn't dream of it. Hello, Auntie," I said as I walked over and kissed her cheek.

"Hello, darling. Did you have a good day at school?"

"I did, thank you, and loads of people send you their love and told me that if either of you need anything, I am to let them know. Harry Patrick also caught me and said that if you wanted him to mow your lawn until you are able to, just let him know."

"That is why I love living in a village!" my uncle replied.

"Now, what is going on in here? You were making a lot of commotion when I arrived."

"Hush, there was no commotion. I was just telling your aunt that I am not an invalid and she needs to take it easy or she will make herself ill."

"I was just making him comfortable. He can be quite stubborn, as you know."

"I have an easy answer to this. Auntie, you sit next to him and relax, and Uncle, do you promise that when you are tired or in pain you will say something? James is just making some tea so we can all relax. Tea is better medicine than anything. You know this, Auntie, as you taught me it. A cup of tea can cure anything."

"I think, May, we have just witnessed teacher Jane. Come on, we'd better do as she says, otherwise we will be given detention."

"I think you might be right," Auntie May responded as she took her place on the sofa next to her husband.

"Did the doctors tell you any more about your condition before they discharged you?" I asked.

"I have to change my diet a little bit. I have some pills to take, and I will need to go back for regular monitoring. But as long as I do as I am told and don't overdo things, I should be fine. There are plenty more years left in me."

Just then, James and Lacy came in with the tea tray.

'See, I told you that you had magic powers," James said to me.

"They said that I was giving them the teacher treatment."

"That would do it. But I'm glad you did. They both needed to calm down."

"Yes, boss," my aunt and uncle responded at the same time, which made us all laugh.

After that, things had calmed down and we managed to get back to being the relaxed family we were, which was just what the doctor ordered, and in no time at all, I realised that it was seven o'clock and I really should leave so that everyone could get on and have dinner, not that they didn't offer me dinner, but I turned them down because of my plans to have a takeaway with David.

I texted David just as I was walking home to let him know I was on my way. He said he would be about an hour, so I had time to freshen up and mark some of the homework that I'd brought home. I also put the plates to warm in the oven. Right on time, David arrived with a meal for two, which we laid out on the coffee table, and we just helped ourselves.

We talked about my day and David's interviews. Apparently, two of the four that were interviewed were what he was looking for, but he only had one vacancy, although he was thinking of taking on both. We also discussed whether or not I had received a flower today. I hadn't. Whilst we shared one of the nicest Indian meals I'd had in a long time, not only did the time fly by but it was also nice to actually talk to someone about my day and the various funny things that the kids had said or done. When I had lived with Peter, he wasn't interested in my day, and on more than one occasion, as soon as I'd started talking about school, he'd walked out of the room. As soon as we finished our meal, David helped to tidy up, and then he set about putting up the new doorbell camera and showing me how to use it, which was quite simple.

Just after 11 o'clock, we both decided to call it a night.

"What are your plans for tomorrow?" I asked.

"I think I have to work tomorrow night, but I will let you know."

"No problem, and thanks again for tonight and putting the doorbell cameras up."

We had another one of the most wonderful kisses that David and I seemed to share.

"I'd better go. I will text you tomorrow. Night night," he said as he turned to go out the door.

"I look forward to it. Night night," I replied, and with that, I turned and locked the door then went to finish my marking. I crawled into bed just after midnight.

David

When I said goodnight to Jane last night, it was hard. I didn't really want to leave her with the knowledge that we still didn't know who was leaving her the flowers, but also because I'd had one of the most relaxing nights I'd had in a long time. It would have been very easy to spend all the free time we had together, but I knew that because her previous relationship had stifled her and stopped her from growing her confidence, I wanted to take it slow so that she could continue to enjoy her independence. I really wanted her to know that I would love a relationship with her but was willing to take the relationship at her speed. First things first: get ready to go to the restaurant.

Apart from yesterday's interviews, I hadn't been there in the last few days. It was the longest break I'd had since I'd opened it.

"Morning, Rebecca," I said as I walked into the restaurant.

"Morning, boss. Sorry I missed you yesterday. How did the interviews go?"

"They went great. Two out of the four I interviewed would work really well here, and they are both local. Even though we only have one vacancy, I think we could offer both of them the job and train them to do front of house, as well as serving the food. That way, we can both take more time off work."

"That's a great idea. Do you mean to say that you are coming round to my way of thinking when it comes to having more time off from the restaurant and leaving your amazing members of staff, me included of course, in charge?"

"Do you know, Rebecca, you really are cheeky. But yes, I am coming round to your way of thinking. But I have developed it and decided that you need to have more time off as well, although you will have to wait a bit longer for your time off. I am, of course, The Boss. Now, time to stop chatting and get on with some work."

"Yes, boss." Just as I heard her say that, I looked back and, sure enough, she was saluting me. Laughing, I walked into my office to start on the paperwork.

I spent most of the morning phoning references for the new staff and contacting interviewees to tell them the outcome. Then at midday, I thought I would text Jane. I knew she probably wouldn't get round to replying before school finished, but if I didn't do it now, I would be in the middle of doing paperwork before I got another chance.

David: Hello, how are you this morning? David xx

I also rang James.

"Hi James, how is your dad?"

"Hi David. Lacy and I got sent away last night. I think he is hoping things can get back to normal, but mum is still a bit shaken up, so she will be forcing him to rest, and she is taking his change in diet very seriously."

"I bet she is. If any of you need anything, just let me know. I wanted you to know, I installed the new doorbell cameras outside Jane's door last night."

"Thank you. Hopefully, we will catch whoever it is putting the flowers there. Is she ok?"

"Yes, I sent a picture of the roses and petals to Connor just in case this escalates even more. The roses and petals, and I think the worry about your dad, became a bit much for her."

"I'm not surprised she didn't tell me, although I think she was more worried about my dad, and I appreciate you telling me and being there for her."

"You know that's not a problem. I like Jane and would do anything for her."

"I know, and the two of you together would make a good

couple, and let's be honest, you are so much better than her ex."

"Thanks. I'd better get on with this paperwork."

"Too right. Bye."

Just as I put my phone down, it buzzed. Taking a look, it was Jane's reply to my text:

Jane: Morning, everything is good, just sitting down for my lunch while I finish my marking.

David: I'm just doing paperwork. Not going to be able to get away tonight, but can tomorrow if you want to come round to mine tomorrow night for dinner?

Jane: That would be lovely. Do you want me to bring anything?

David: Just yourself. But will you promise me that if you are left any gifts, you will let me know?

Jane: I will, I promise. See you tomorrow, I look forward to it.

David: Likewise.

Now that was sorted out, I set out getting the big pile of paperwork down. I had just finished sending emails to the people I interviewed the other day when my mobile rang again. Taking a look at the caller, I saw that it was Stephanie, my ex-wife. I decided I didn't want to deal with her and her dramas, so I ignored her call. As I walked to the kitchen to get myself a sandwich, I realised that Jane was so different to Stephanie. I tried to think of the reason why my younger self married her. Maybe I was just blinded by the person she tried to portray herself to be?

The rest of the day went by quite quickly, and the evening service in the restaurant, although it ran smoothly with no complaints, was busy with the two sittings we had and one private function happening. It was all hands on deck, and even Rebecca was having to clear tables as I was on back up bar duty. Before I left for home, I thought I would message Jane as I hadn't heard from her all night, and just as I picked up my phone, I realised I hadn't listened to the voicemail Stephanie had left. I was too tired to listen to it, and I doubted there was anything she could say that was important enough for me to listen to. It could wait.

David: Are you awake?

Jane: I am.

As soon as I got the text confirming that she was awake, I decided to phone her.

"Hi, I didn't want to ring you too late, but I was just getting ready to leave the restaurant and wanted to check you were ok."

"That's ok, I was just finishing off the book I was reading before I go to sleep."

"I take it you haven't received any gifts today?"

"No, I haven't received anything. That's two days running, so hopefully it has stopped."

"Hopefully. How was school today? I hope they were still behaving themselves."

"They were, which made it a lot easier, not that they are ever that naughty. There are just times when you wonder what food they have been eating as they are all so hyperactive and hard to settle down. Did everything work as well as you hoped in the restaurant tonight?"

"Yes, it did. Everyone seemed to have a great time, and I know that the waiting staff got some good tips as well. But I am exhausted. It's been ages since I've worked in the bar for the whole night."

"I totally understand. Every now and then, especially when James had just taken over the pub, I had to work behind the bar, which was fun but very tiring. Actually, that reminds me, he still owes me for that. I bet he thinks I've forgotten."

"I'd better let you get to bed. I'm looking forward to tomorrow night."

"So am I. Night, David."

"Night, sweet dreams."

Just as I was saying goodnight, Rebecca came into the office.

"Sweet dreams, is it boss? I've never seen you like this before."

"Do you want something or did you just come in to tease me?"

"No. That's an added bonus. I wanted to tell you that everything is tidy, and I have let everyone leave, so I am just about to go now."

"Great, thanks, do you want a lift?"

"Actually, I wouldn't say no if it's not too much trouble. My feet are killing me tonight. At least tomorrow night will be quieter."

Still talking, we walked through the restaurant, locking up on the way out to the car.

The drive didn't take long, which is usual for the village, and twenty minutes later, I entered my house, looking over the rooms to see what I needed to do in the way of tidying up before Jane came tomorrow. For the first time in a long time, I was glad I had been at work so much because the house didn't need that much tidying. Not that I was a slob, but I couldn't even remember the last time I had actually cooked a meal in my house. Most of my meals, apart from the ones I'd had with Jane, had been at the restaurant. I got the chicken out from the freezer ready to defrost for tomorrow night, then I went to bed. I was done in.

Chapter 7

David

I hoovered before I went to work, and I was glad that I did as it would save a lot of time as I was delayed at work and didn't manage to get away as quick as I hoped I would. I came back armed with the groceries I needed to make chicken pasta bake and some lovely fresh fruit for a fruit salad for dessert, if it was required. It wasn't exactly the most complicated recipe in the world, but I wanted to have something simple that just needed to finish off in the oven. I had just managed to get into the kitchen with the shopping when my phone started ringing, and, because I was distracted trying to deal with the shopping, I didn't look at the screen to see who was ringing.

"Hello?"

"David, is that you?"

With those four words I realised how stupid I had been not looking at the caller ID.

"Of course it is, who did you expect it to be? What do you want, Stephanie?"

"Don't be like that, David. I left you a message yesterday.

Did you not get it?"

"I did get it, but I haven't listened to it yet. I have been busy. What do you want?"

"I wondered if we could meet up."

"No, we can't. We are divorced and I don't want to see you again. Goodbye."

I put the phone down, my heart pumping with irritation. I really did wish I hadn't answered it in the first place. Hopefully, cooking the dinner would relax me enough that Jane and I could have a nice night and I could put that phone call behind me. No sooner had I put the dinner in the oven and chopped up the fruit for the fruit salad than the doorbell went.

"Right on time," I said to her as I moved to welcome her with a kiss on the lips.

"Hi, I know you said I didn't need to bring anything, but I thought I would bring some drinks. I know you like this beer, but I also bought some white wine as well."

"Thank you, come in." I moved away from the door, and as she came into the house, I put my hand at the small of her back to guide her and reassure her that there was no need to be nervous. Her back was ram rod straight, and even where my hand was at her lower back, I could feel the tension running through her. She wasn't the only one who was nervous. I was worried about what she would think of my house. Her house had character and was lovely and homely, whereas mine was more functional, mainly because I hadn't spent much time there because I was at the restaurant so much. My living room was quite bare compared to hers. I had a brown leather sofa and a big television on a glass cabinet, but, other than a few pictures on the white walls, it really was plain. Unlike Jane's house, my house had an open plan kitchen, dining and living room. I had set the table for tonight, but I wanted to get her comfortable and there was still a few minutes before dinner was ready.

"Are you ok? Did something happen? You seem a bit tense," I asked her.

"Yes, no, nothing has happened. I'm sorry, I guess I am just nervous, although I don't know why. It's not as if we haven't eaten together before."

"That's true, although this is the first time you have come to my place, and that probably makes it feel like a real date. Or is it because you are worried about my cooking?" I said, trying to lighten the mood.

"You're probably right, at least about the date thing. But I doubt someone who owns one of the best restaurants in the area is a lousy chef."

"I hope I'm not, although the only person I want to impress tonight is you. Let me take your jacket. Why don't you sit on the sofa? It is one of the most comfortable places in here! Dinner will be about twenty minutes. Would you like a drink?" Pausing to take a breath, I realised that I had just bombarded her with questions and information.

"Wow, I guess I'm not the only one who is nervous tonight."

"Guilty as charged. But at least you're not alone."

"A drink would be lovely. I'll have whatever you're having."

Hanging her jacket up on the coat hook in the hall, I went to the kitchen and poured her a glass of wine before taking a deep breath to try to calm myself.

"Here you are. How was your day today?"

"Thank you, it actually wasn't too bad. I managed to work out who was going to do what in the annual school concert so that even the musically challenged child gets to shine. Although I am sure you don't want to be bored with the details."

"Actually, I'm interested. When I was in school, I had this music teacher, and you remind me of her. She was really good. Her opinion was that everyone can sing. They just can't sing every song. But there is a song for everyone out there."

"That's what I think. I love music and the positives it can

have on life, and just like there is a song for every event, there is a song for every person. I love talking about my work, but I want you to promise to tell me if you get bored of me talking about it. Peter used to hate me telling him about my work."

"I am not Peter, and I could never get bored listening to you talk about your work. When you talk about it your face lights up. Why would anyone want to dim that?"

Just as I was saying that the timer on the oven went off.

"That's dinner. I hope chicken pasta bake is acceptable. Come over to the table and I will bring the dinner out and we can talk more about your work while you sample my wares."

"That sounds lovely."

It felt like the meal went quickly as we discussed Jane's love of teaching and mine of cooking. Before I knew it, the plates were cleared of all food and the wine bottle was empty.

"Thank you so much, that was a wonderful meal." Jane looked at me, smiling.

"No problem. Anytime."

"Oh, don't say that. I will be knocking on your door every day for dinner."

"I wouldn't mind that. Now you stay there and I will clear the table." I got up, and as I reached for her plate, I gave her a quick kiss.

With the table cleared and the dishwasher loaded, I was just about to ask her if I could get her anything else when she asked me, "I didn't realise the time! Would you think me rude if I left to go home? I have an early morning tomorrow."

"Not at all. In fact, why don't I walk you home? That way I will know that you got home safe and sound."

"As long as you're sure. I don't want to put you out."

"It would be a pleasure to escort a beautiful lady home."

"Thank you."

With our jackets on, we walked hand in hand through the village from my house to hers, with Jane pointing out places of interest from her childhood, including the place where her mother had taught her to ride a bike and where, a couple of seconds later, she had fallen off that bike. I could tell by the way her face lit up that she had very fond memories of her mum and that she missed her a lot. I knew that was the reason why she was so close to her aunt.

"I would love to have another date with you, but I'm not sure when I can next get a night off," I said. "I will go to your aunt's house on Saturday for her barbeque, and I would love to take you as well."

"That would be wonderful. I can't think of anyone I would rather go with. I knew you had been invited. I think my aunt is secretly hoping you will step in and do the cooking, although it is just a small affair this time. Family and their closest friends."

"I don't mind doing the cooking. In fact, I offered. I've had a barbeque cooked by James and only just lived to tell the tale, so for the safety of everyone, I thought it was best."

We were laughing as we reached her door, and I was relieved to find that there was nothing left on her doorstep.

"Would you like to come in?" Jane said.

"No, I'd better not. If I did, you definitely wouldn't be getting an early night." I grabbed her other hand and wrapped myself around her, giving her one of our explosive signature kisses. It was only broken up when I heard someone shout in a humorous way, "Get a room!" followed by a laugh. I rested my forehead on hers as we both tried to breathe. As soon as we had regained some kind of normality, we both started laughing, and I noticed she had gone bright red.

"Do you know who that was?" I said.

"Yes, I do, and I know that before you get home the

village will be up to date on what my old teacher Mrs Baker just witnessed. She is friends with my aunt and her friend Lily, and like them she may be retired but she still has a sense of humour. I hope that's ok with you."

"Of course it is. I would class it as an honour if I was connected with you romantically and for everyone to know that we are together, as long as you agree. I don't want to push you into a relationship with me, especially after everything you have had to go through with Peter."

"I don't know what to say to that other than thank you. The feeling is mutual. I would rather put Peter behind me. I have wasted too much time on him."

"Good. You'd better go inside before I weaken and come inside like you offered. I'll speak to you tomorrow."

"I look forward to it." She gave me a chaste kiss on the lips then went inside, and I waited until I heard the door lock before I left.

The next day was busy at the restaurant, but I still managed to get a chance to text Jane and find out how her day was going and let her know that I had managed to get Saturday off. I asked if she wanted to go out for the day before we went to May's house. I could pick her up at twelve o'clock and we could have lunch somewhere.

We exchanged a few texts for the rest of the week, but I hadn't managed to get any time off. So, on Saturday, just before midday, I knocked on her door. I hadn't really organised much to do, but as it was a nice day, one of the options I had thought of was to have lunch at the pub and then take a walk along the river and up to the chapel. I hadn't managed to visit it until now, but, as it overlooked the village, I knew it was there. Ringing her doorbell and waiting for Jane to answer had me second guessing myself as to what we would do.

Just as the doubts entered my head, Jane answered the door. "Morning, come in. I won't be long, I'm just finishing off in the kitchen."

"Morning. I wasn't sure what you wanted to do today, so I haven't organised anything, but I thought as it's a nice day, we could have lunch and go for a walk?"

"Great minds think alike. I hope you don't mind, but I thought I would make a picnic rather than having food inside. I thought on a day like this we could eat outside and get some fresh air."

Looking at all the food on the workbench I wasn't sure that I would be able to eat it all!

"That's an excellent idea. Looking at all this food is making me hungry."

"It's just a few basic things I have put together. Nothing special."

"It will be lovely. Are you ready to go?

"I just need to put the dishwasher on and then I will be ready."

Five minutes later, we left her house. Carrying the picnic bag in one hand and holding Jane's hand in the other, I felt happy and at peace. For the first time in a long time, I wasn't worrying about the restaurant and what else I needed to do to rebuild my life after the divorce.

"Have you ever walked along the canal to the hill with the old chapel on the top?" she asked. "It might be a nice place to have lunch, especially after walking up the hill. The view is out of this world."

Smiling at her, I replied, "I have never done that. I have of course seen the chapel and wanted to visit it, but I haven't had a lot of time off from the restaurant until lately. You might have to push me up the hill!"

"I have walked up that hill a few times, and trust me, there is no way I'm helping you. You're on your own. When we were kids, James and I and our friends used to run up that hill on a daily basis and in all weathers, but the older I get the more I wonder what happened to the energy I had back then. But you're in luck because I know an easier way to get up there."

"Thank heavens I'm with you, then! Lead the way."

It took about ten minutes to walk along the river and get to the bottom of the hill. Every time I looked up it, the steep climb seemed to grow, the hill getting higher with my every grimace. Due to the last part of the path being narrow, I had to let go of Jane's hand. When I turned around to ask her if she was ready for the climb, she had disappeared.

Looking around I couldn't see her, and just as I was about to panic, I heard her say, "Are you coming, slow coach? I promise you, the view is better from the top."

Following Jane towards what she promised was an easier way up the hill and moving away from the towpath, I saw some steep steps, about 20 in total, and at the top on the right-hand side I could see a house and on the left a tarmacked path. Luckily, the steps were evenly placed and well-maintained, so it was easy to walk up. Although tiring, I certainly felt like my thigh muscles were getting a workout, but just as I could feel the burn, we reached the top. Jane didn't even look out of breath. I obviously needed to up my exercise routine ... or maybe even start it.

"Wow, that was a workout. Are you sure this is an easier way to the top?"

"I guess I found it easy because I'm used to it. It's definitely easier than the other way, but if you want, when we come down, we can go the other way and see which you prefer."

"You're the boss. Maybe I need to spend less time in the restaurant and more time out and about getting fresh air, then the hill wouldn't seem to be much of a challenge! I take it we go left now unless we turn right and pop into that house for a cup of tea."

"Yes, we turn left, and it's just up this road. We could pop in for a cup of tea, but that house belongs to Lily, and I know she is spending the day with Auntie May."

"Lead the way."

She was right. When we made it up to the top of the hill, standing on the top of the hill was the wonderful, with the ruined chapel that overlooked the village up close. It certainly looked impressive, and the view of the village was amazing. Walking over to one side, I could see so much of the village from where we were standing. Looking out at the view, I felt Jane come up to stand by me.

"Wow. You weren't kidding when you said there is no other view than the one from up here."

"I know. It's amazing. James and I use to come up here a lot with our friends. It was like a secret world, although everyone knew about it, and I'm sure when my mum was a child, she used to come up here with her friends, as well. It wasn't as if we were getting up to anything naughty, it was just nice to be away from the village for a while and be able to do anything without it getting back to our parents."

"I bet James played a lot of football up here. That's the only thing I can see him getting into trouble for."

"You know him so well. I lost count of how many balls he kicked over the hill, although he did used to roll down the hill to get them. My aunt used to be forever telling him off for the state of his clothes."

Jane walked around to find a flat place to lay the blanket. There weren't any trees around so there was nowhere we could go for shade. The grass was short, which showed that someone was looking after this beautiful quiet place. As soon as she found a place, she asked, "Shall we put the blanket down here?"

"Yes, this would be a perfect place."

Sitting on the blanket and getting the food out of the bag, I was just about to eat a sandwich when I asked Jane to tell me more of her memories.

"I am lucky I have so many good memories. I think this was down to the fact that I knew I was loved even though my dad wasn't around. I knew I had my aunt and uncle to rely on. When my mum worked, Auntie May used to look after me, and when she was working, my mum used to look after James. Our friends were always welcome to join us even if we were going out for the day. No one was turned away. What was your childhood like?"

"I was a typical only child. I lived with my mum and dad. I tended not to get into trouble. I spent more time reading and with my mum in the kitchen. She was an amazing cook, and she was the one who taught me how to cook. I wasn't really into sports like football. I preferred running. My mum and dad died when I was at university with James, and just after, I met my now ex-wife. A year later, I married her, which was the biggest mistake of my life."

After we'd finished talking about our memories, we looked around the chapel on the hill. I had done a bit of research about the church when James had first mentioned I should visit it, so I already knew it was a 14th Century Chapel, but I hadn't expected the ruin to be so beautiful. There wasn't much left apart from the outer shell of the main church, with the bell tower still intact. The roof was gone, and the internal decorations of the chapel were missing. Despite that, you could still see some of the original features, including the arched windows.

"We'd better get a move on. We haven't got much time left before we need to be at your aunt's. Let's try the other way down!" I said.

"I have half a mind to let you go down the other way on your own. But I am all about challenges, and I do want to see your face when you realise that I was right about this being the harder way. But just take it easy, because sometimes before you know it you will start running down the hill instead of walking because it is steeper than you think."

Walking down the hill to start with was not so bad, but just as we were used to walking downwards at an angle slowly, I suddenly realised that I was running down the hill. Looking back to make sure that Jane was ok, I saw that instead of walking straight down behind me, she was walking in almost a zig zag pattern. Although she looked tense, her back was upright over her bent knees. Obviously, this had helped her from being taken down the hill due to the momentum. Getting nearer the bottom, I started worrying about whether or not I would be able to stop myself moving before I fell into the river. Luckily, I found that as soon as I reached the bottom, I had more control, but very wobbly legs. I was glad there was a bench where I could sit down for a minute. Jane came round the corner and sat next to me.

"Did you enjoy that?"

"Not really, no." I laughed. "You were right, the way we went up was far easier. But you could have given me more tips on how to get down without nearly falling in the river!"

"I could have done, but where would the fun in that be?" She nudged my shoulder with hers and laughed.

"You'll pay for that. Come on, we'd better go. Hopefully my legs will hold me up now, and while we're walking back, you can tell me the tricks of walking down a steep hill."

We had a leisurely walk back. Honestly, I could not have done a fast-paced walk just then if my life had depended on it. When we got to May's house, Jane let us in.

Jane

As soon as we got to my aunt's house, David went straight to the outside grill and started making sure everything was lit whilst talking to my uncle and James. In the meantime, I was talking to Lacy about where we had been. Lacy excused herself to get another drink, and while she was gone, I looked at David, thinking. Honestly, I wasn't sure I was actually looking at *him*. I was really staring off into space.

"Are you alright, darling?" my aunt surprised me by asking. I didn't realise I was no longer alone.

"Yes, I actually am, Auntie."

"Good, you should be. How are you and David getting on?"

"We are good. I was just thinking how easy it is being with

David. He actually seems to enjoy my company. He is constantly doing small things for me; like the other day, I mentioned to Lacy on the phone when David was around that one of the bushes out the front was getting a bit big, and the next thing I knew, he was standing outside with a hedge trimmer in his hands. He knows more about me in this short time than Peter ever did, which is sad as we knew each other since school. We have a laugh, but we can talk about the serious stuff as well."

"That is who you need in your life. Someone who will treat you as if you are important to them. Someone who knows the real you."

"Anyway, how are you?"

"I am slowly getting over the shock. I know it was your uncle who was unwell, but he has never been unwell like that before, and I think it just made me realise that he is not indestructible."

"He will be alright. I think he just thought that he needed to spice things up for a little while. You know him. When he sets out to do things, he does them so well."

"He really does. Anyway, I told him I don't need that kind of excitement in my life. I think David is trying to get our attention."

Just as she said that I heard David shout, "Food's ready,

everyone. Come and get it before James does."

"Hey!" James replied good naturedly.

Placing the food out on a big table, the six of us sat around eating and laughing, normally at James' expense. By the time everyone had finished, the sky was starting to get dark, so, after helping to tidy up, David and I decided to call it a night and walked back to my house.

After such a relaxing and carefree day, I was horrified to realise that, as soon as we got to my doorstep, I could see another rose. It had been a few days since I had last received one, and I had thought it had ended. Like the others, there was no note, but at least this time hopefully we would be able to see who had left it there. Stepping over the rose and leaving it there, David and I went into my house, and I went to get my laptop so that we could see if the camera had caught the culprit. Going through the video, as soon as I saw who it was who had left the roses, I could not believe what I was seeing.

"That's Peter isn't it?" David asked, looking at me with concern.

"I can't believe this. He never bought me a rose in all the time we were in a relationship. Why now, and why just leave them with no note?"

"I don't know." David looked so angry, he stood up and

started pacing backwards and forwards with his hand balled into a fist as he tried to calm himself down. Sitting back down next to me and holding my hand, he continued, "On the plus side, we know who it is now. But what do you want to do about this?"

"I have an idea, but first I think we need to get James and Lacy here so that I can tell you all at the same time. You're right, it makes it a little bit easier to know who it was."

"Ok, you stay there and I will phone James and see if they are free."

I decided, while David was talking to James, that I would screenshot the pictures of Peter leaving the rose so that I could have them developed in case I needed them for evidence. Getting up to make a cup of decaf coffee, for us both, David put his arms around me and pulled me so that I was tightly tucked in between him and the workbench with my back to his chest. He kissed me on the top of my head.

"James said they were just about to leave your aunt's place, so they will be about ten minutes. He also said he will have a coffee and Lacy will have a peppermint tea. How are you holding up?"

Turning round and looking up at him, I replied, "Actually, I'm ok. I know that's an odd thing to say because of how frightening these gifts have been but I'm glad I know who it is now, and hopefully this will be over soon. And I am *so* happy that you're here with me."

"There is nowhere I would rather be than by your side."

I kissed him, and just as we were starting to get carried away, the kettle clicked off. Turning away from David, I set about making everyone's drinks, and just as we got them through to the living room, the doorbell rang. David answered the door, and James came through and gave me a hug, and then Lacy asked me if I was alright. Nodding to her, we went and sat down on the sofa as I showed James the video. I thought David was angry, but James seemed to have steam coming out of his ears, and I think if Lacy hadn't been holding onto him, I would have worried about what he was going to do when he caught up with Peter. I knew he wouldn't be happy when hearing what I wanted to do about it.

Just as I was about to tell him to calm down, he said, "Right, Lacy, you stay here with Jane. Jane, I don't want you to worry about it. David and I will go and find Peter and have a few words with him. We will get this sorted now."

"You will do no such thing. I stopped needing you to fight my battles years ago, and I have already decided what I am going to do. So sit down, shut up, and listen," I snapped. James complied with a sheepish look on his face. "I have given it some thought, and I have decided that I am going to fight this battle on my own; well, nearly on my own. I was wondering if we could have a word with Connor and see if he would be available to pop round in an unofficial capacity to sit there while I talk to Peter. I don't want you involved, James. I know you, and so does he. If he is put in a corner, which he will be, because he won't be expecting picture evidence, he will press your buttons, and then you will explode and he will have won."

"I hate it when you're the sensible one. You're right, but I don't like it. Do you want me to phone Connor? He owes me a favour anyway."

"Thank you, yes please."

James nodded and went into the kitchen to phone Connor. David asked me if I was sure this was the way I wanted to do it, and I when I reassured him, I knew then that he supported me and respected me enough to trust me. Just then, James shouted out that Connor could come over tonight if I wanted him to. I agreed that I would love that, and it was arranged that he would come round in half an hour and I would tell Peter to come round in an hour as I wanted to talk to him. That would give us time to talk through the action plan. Having finished our drinks, it was agreed that James and Lacy would leave but I would phone them as soon as Peter left. David asked me if I wanted him to stay or go. I really wanted him to stay, so I asked him if he would mind staying in one of the other rooms with the door closed so that Peter didn't know he was there. I knew after I had confronted Peter that I would need David to calm me down. Just as James and Lacy left, Connor arrived. I had known Connor all my life; he was one of James' friends at school. He used to be a small, thin little boy, but he had really grown up. He was now over six foot tall, and I knew that he really liked taking part in triathlons in his spare time. You could tell, especially as he was wearing a t-shirt which showed off his biceps. Nothing else had changed about him, he still had his focused grey eyes and auburn hair.

After making Connor a tea, I went through my plan with him and David. I wanted David to stay out of sight as I thought his presence might antagonise Peter. I wanted Connor not to say anything unless he needed to. As far as I was concerned, and I think Connor agreed, he wasn't here in an official police role, but I hoped it might make Peter stand up and think about what he had done. I didn't want to get back with him. Having spent the time with David, as soon as this was sorted out, I couldn't wait to see where things would go with him. But first, I needed this sorted.

Just as I had thought, my doorbell went, and, as I had left my laptop connected and on, we saw it was Peter. David checked in with me again to make sure I was definite that I was ok with this. He gave me a quick kiss before he went into my room and closed the door. Taking a deep breath and pasting a smile on my face, I opened the front door to be faced with what I could only describe as Peter wearing a wide grin as if he had won the lottery. I would soon be wiping that smile off his face.

"Come in," I told him as he walked past me. He tried to give me a kiss, but I moved my face as soon as I saw him coming towards me. I saw a glimpse of shock when he couldn't believe I wasn't following some unsaid plan he had made up.

It didn't take him long to bounce back. "Alright, darling." Walking towards the living room, he stopped as soon as he got to the doorway. I assumed that was when he saw Connor. Although I would have loved to see his face, seeing him look so hesitant was just as good.

"In you go. You know Connor, don't you? I don't know if you have heard, he has just been promoted and is now working at our police station."

Taking a minute to clear the tension, I heard him say, "Hi, Connor. I didn't know you were going to be here."

"Oh, don't mind me. Just pretend I'm not here," Connor replied.

Sitting down in the chair, I left the sofa to Peter. I didn't want to be stuck with him sitting next to me.

"Take a seat, Peter," I said.

"I don't know what's going on. How do you expect us to restart our relationship and for me to forgive you with Connor here?"

"Well, give me a moment to explain what's going on." I paused to take a breath. "Our relationship will never be restarted. You and I are over. I found you in my bed with Sarah!" I paused and took another breath. I needed to be calm, not angry. "But if I hadn't caught you, I would still be listening to your self-centred tripe and putting up with your disinterest in me and my life. So, thank you for helping me see the light."

Before he could say anything, and after I took another breath and tried to steady by shaking hands, I continued. "I don't know what you are playing at with the roses and the little gifts you have been leaving on my doorstep, but you need to stop. You might not know this, but it could be classed as stalking, and as such, I am well within my rights to inform the police. However, I won't if it stops now. But if there are any more gifts, I have witnesses and evidence that it was you leaving them, and I will report it and follow through, starting with the restraining order that I told your brother I would get the last time you showed up here drunk. I meant it then and I mean it now. You need to get it in your thick head that I am not interested. That ship has sailed, and you have lost the best thing you ever had. Am I making myself clear?"

I'd always thought the saying 'stream coming out of his ears' was a bit silly ... until now. I could imagine the sound and visualise his head about to explode. Looking towards Connor, he gave me a quick smile, which helped to reassure me that I was safe. Although Peter had never been violent towards me, his behaviour lately had changed so much. I think that if I had been on my own, I wouldn't feel safe.

Eventually, Peter spoke. "Where is this coming from? Why don't we get rid of Connor so I can talk to you properly? I don't understand why you are so annoyed. I made a little mistake, but that shouldn't make you so angry, and I am not harassing you, I just wanted to know when I was moving back."

"You really need to listen, Peter. If anyone is leaving, it is you. And Connor is staying. I will tell you again, and then I want you to leave, and I never want to see you again. And if you won't leave, then I will phone the police and have you removed from the property. We are not getting back together - not now and not ever. Now go and leave me alone. Connor, would you mind showing Peter out?"

Connor got up and did exactly that. As I watched a shocked Peter leave, I took a deep breath. Hopefully it would all be over and done with now. Connor must have said something to Peter as well, because it took a while before he came back into the living room, with David following him. As I was still standing by the couch, David came towards me and put his arms around me, pulling me towards him. It was only then that I realised I was shaking.

Reassuring me, David whispered, "I am so proud of you," whilst he rubbed his hand reassuringly up and down my back. David helped me sit on the sofa as Connor came in with a cup of peppermint tea for me.

"Thank you so much, Connor. I couldn't have done that without you."

"Nonsense," he told me. "I don't think you will hear from him again. But if you do, I want you to phone the station straight away."

"I will. Thank you so much."

"No problem, you did really well, Jane. Don't get up, I will let myself out."

"He's right, you know. You did really well," David said as the front door closed behind Connor. "I am so proud of you. I may have had James on speakerphone so that he could listen to you handle things. I think he was blown away by how strong you were. Although why that should surprise him, I don't know. But he was trying to find the right words to describe what he thought of you, and all he kept saying was "wow" over and over again. I think you struck him dumb!"

"Thank you for being here with me. I think you and Connor being here gave me the strength. I just can't understand when Peter became such an entitled, selfish being. But you, along with everyone else, have told me that I deserve better. Would you mind staying tonight? I don't know what you have planned tomorrow, but I have had a wonderful day and I don't want it to end."

"I would love to stay. I don't have anything planned for tomorrow."

Making sure the house was locked up before David and I went into my bedroom just felt natural. There was no expectation. Everything just moved along as naturally as it could.

When we got into my room, David said to me, "I want you to relax and put everything out of your mind. The only thing that matters now is getting a good night's sleep." He sealed those wise words with a kiss, which continued as we explored each other's bodies with slow touches, discovering each of our reactions. I didn't know whether it was due to the release of all the stress I had been under or if it was just being with David, but I had never thought of myself as being a sensual person until then.

Eventually, we stopped, and David whispered, "Not tonight. Soon, but not tonight."

I knew exactly what he was referring to, and although I could understand the sense in not making love tonight, I wasn't really sure I appreciated it. After we eventually separated, we both went through our bedtime routines and went to bed doing nothing but cuddling.

That night it was easy to fall asleep wrapped up in his arms. Him wearing his boxer shorts and me wearing my t-shirt nightie. It was one of the best sleeps I'd had for a long time. I think knowing who was leaving the roses for me took a lot of worry off my shoulders. At last, I felt free from everything I had been worrying about.

When I woke up, I quietly got out of bed, hoping not to disturb David, and went to make him a cup of coffee and put some bacon in the oven for sandwiches. Just as the coffee machine had finished, David walked into the kitchen and treated me to one of his amazing kisses. Now that was a good way to wake up in the morning.

"Morning, gorgeous," he said.

"Morning. I have some bacon in the oven for some sandwiches if that's ok for breakfast?"

"That's great. You should have woken me up. I don't

expect you to wait on me hand and foot."

"I know you don't, but you looked cute fast asleep. I was watching you for a bit before I got up, and you looked so peaceful that I thought it was best to let you sleep."

"Cute? I'll give you cute!" With that, he tickled me, and it would appear that I was very ticklish. In the end, I was crying for mercy before he stopped.

"Do you take that back? I am not cute!" he said as he cuddled me and kissed my forehead.

"Ok, I take that back! You're not cute. But you'd better let me go before we have very burnt bacon for breakfast."

"If I must," he said, tapping me on the bottom as I turned around.

As we sat down to breakfast, I realised that we were so relaxed in each other's company that the silences were not awkward and any conversations just flowed. David had some things to do at home and I had some marking and clothes washing to do, so we decided to meet up at 4 o'clock and then decide where we could go for dinner or whether or not we should have it at home.

Time went by quickly as I concentrated on marking the workbooks I had brought home whilst I put about three loads of washing on. Just as I got the last load out of the dryer, I heard a knock on the door, and that was when I realised it was four o'clock.

"Hi, come in."

"Thank you," David said and wandered in, then lent down to give me a kiss.

Walking into the living room, I excused myself to go and get the rest of the washing out of the dryer. I was starting to fold it up, ready to go in the basket to be put away, when David came and joined me.

"Let me help with that. There's no point in me sitting there doing nothing when I could be helping you instead."

"Thank you. I did hope I would be done now, but James phoned up and then I had a phone call from Auntie May, so things took longer than I thought."

"Was James still speechless?"

"He said 'welcome back'. I think that's his roundabout way of saying I was a doormat for far too long and he is proud of me. Like me, he doesn't understand how or what made Peter change from the person he once was, but he is glad he is out of my life now."

"And were your aunt and uncle alright after the barbecue yesterday?"

"Yes, they were. In fact, my aunt says anytime you want to cook, just let her know, and Uncle Mike says he's not sure he can do the cooking again after you showed him up!"

It didn't take long for the two of us to fold the washing, and after making us both a drink, we went into the living room to discuss what we were going to do about dinner. In the end, David said he wanted to take me out for dinner to celebrate the end of the case of the anonymous rose deliverer, but we didn't want to go too far, so we settled for just going to the pub. I did warn David that if we went to the pub we wouldn't remain just the two of us for long as there was bound to be someone we knew there wanting a quick chat, but he said he was ok with that. As usual, David was wearing a smart shirt, but I wanted to have a quick shower and change as I felt grubby after doing the day's chores. We didn't leave the house until just after six, and that was with me hurrying as well. By the time we got to the pub, it was busy, with the football club members drinking, all of whom I had known since childhood. After having a quick laugh with them and a chat with some of the women in the pub, David found us a table. Having placed our order, I was just settling down when Peter's brother, Stephen, came over.

"Jane, can I say how sorry I am about Peter's behaviour? If I had known what he was doing, I would have tried to stop him."

"Oh, Stephen, don't be silly. There is nothing for you to apologise for. He was the one who was the idiot, and there is nothing you or your family could do about it. I would like to introduce you to David. He owns the restaurant by the river. David, this is Peter's brother, Stephen. He is definitely the better brother."

"It's nice to meet you, Stephen. Would you like to join us?" David asked. Stephen seemed taken aback by the offer but managed to cover up the shock on his face quickly. "Thank you for the offer, but no, you carry on with your date. You don't need a third wheel sitting with you. I just wanted to apologise again."

"What are you apologising for? If you're apologising for your brother's behaviour, you and I are going to fall out." I heard my cousin's voice before I saw him.

Carrying a pint of beer and a glass of wine, presumably for Lacy, James sat down at our table.

'Sit down, why don't you, James?" David said with a touch of humour.

"Thanks, I will. Here, you sit down next to me, Stephen. That way you won't be a third wheel. But I warn you, Lacy is around, so that will make you a fifth wheel.

"Where is Lacy?" I asked.

"The football lads have got her and won't let her go, apparently. They want to talk to her about organising an event to raise money for them. They want to have it as well as their annual dinner and awards presentation.

"Now, what were we discussing? Oh yes. Stephen, I hope Jane has told you that none of us blame you or your parents for your stupid brother's mistakes and behaviour, so you can stop feeling guilty. And tell that to your mother as well, otherwise I will get May to pop round and tell her."

"Thank you, James, I really appreciate it. As far as I'm concerned, this was the last straw. Peter needs to sort his life out; preferably away from here."

"Right, I propose a toast, forgetting Peter the idiot," I said. The entire pub seemed to respond with, "Here here". As I looked over to the other tables, I saw Lily and all her friends, including my old head teacher, who had spotted me kissing David on the doorstep only a few days ago.

Lily called over to me, "Good riddance to bad rubbish!", and everyone on the two tables laughed, including Stephen.

Eventually, Lacy came over, and the five of us sat chatting and eating until it was chucking out time.

"Thank you for a great night. It was lovely to meet you, David. Please make Jane as happy as she deserves to be,"

Stephen said before kissing both me and Lacy on the cheeks and shaking David's and James' hands.

"I will do, don't you worry about that. See you soon," replied David.

With that, the five of us left the pub and all went our separate ways; Stephen to his car, Lacy and James turning towards her house, and David and I walking to mine. "Thank you for tonight, it was a wonderful evening. And thank you for making Stephen so welcome. Being Peter's brother has never been easy for him as they are so different, and Stephen takes on too much responsibility for the way Peter behaves, which is stupid as he's younger than Peter."

"It was a good night, and I enjoyed meeting Stephen. It isn't his fault his brother is an idiot. It was a nice relaxing night and great to have some laughs after all the stress you have been under."

Just as I was about to reply, his phone rang. He took it out of his pocket, looked at the screen, then put it back in his pocket.

"Did you want to answer that?"

"No, it will only ruin our perfect night; they can leave a message, and I will deal with them later."

"Ok, if you're sure. I would love it if you wanted to come in."

"It would be nice to say goodbye without your old head teacher spying on us."

"Have you not got over that yet?"

"I was doing ok at putting it to the back of my mind until your aunt cornered me at the barbeque and told me that Joan had phoned to ask her to pass on a message."

Laughing, I replied, "Oh, and what was the message?"

"That she approves of your taste in men now! But we might find it more comfortable, erm, talking indoors."

"Ha ha, well at least you have her seal of approval. Come on then, we'd better do what she says."

Still laughing at the mortified look on his face, I unlocked my front door and let us in.

No sooner had I got the door closed than David grabbed me, turning around so that we were facing each other, and he preceded to take my breath away by giving me one of his earth-shattering kisses. It felt like it ended to soon when he finally lifted his head up and said, "I have wanted to do that all night, but I didn't think it was appropriate in front of everyone."

"You're probably right, but if I had known, I would have called it an early night."

"I think you should just assume that whenever you are near me, I want to kiss you and touch you."

"Snap. Do you want to stay? I have to be up early tomorrow as we have a staff meeting starting at eight."

"I would love to, but I also have an early morning, so I'd better go, as unlike you, I need my beauty sleep."

"You say the best things."

"I not only say them, I mean them."

After another kiss or two, he left.

David

I couldn't believe that Stephanie had phoned again. I thought I had made myself clear that I didn't want to have anything to do with her after all this time. Now that my life was sorted out, with the restaurant being able to hold its own, without me working hundreds of hours a day, and now that Jane had sorted out Peter and we could concentrate on our relationship, I was beginning to enjoy life again. By the time I got home, I decided I wasn't going to worry about it anymore. As I told Jane earlier, I didn't want it to spoil the evening.

Walking into my house, I put my phone on to charge in the living room and got ready for bed. I was trying to test the theory of 'out of sight, out of mind'. It must have worked because I didn't think any more about the message left for me as my dreams were taken up by a strong independent woman who showed people that she was no doormat. Waking up in the morning was usually hard for me as I was normally so exhausted by the work that needed doing in the restaurant. But not today. I woke up feeling invigorated. After putting the coffee machine on, my first task was to text Jane.

"Morning, beautiful. I hope you had a good sleep?"

"Morning. I did, thank you. Did you?"

"I did. I was dreaming about this independent, strong, beautiful woman I know."

"Well, tell her to get out of your head. That's my place."

"Oh, you have nothing to fear. It was definitely you in my head."

"Good, but I'd better go, otherwise I will be late. I'll ring you when I finish work, but don't worry if you're busy. You can ring me back."

"Ok, speak to you later, and have a good day xx"

"You to xx"

After that, I decided to concentrate as well as I could with work, and to start off with, I had a meeting with all my staff to introduce the new members, although in Greengrove that wasn't normally needed because everyone knew everyone else. But I usually did it so that I could get some important bulletins out to everyone. We had a couple of small functions coming up, but other than that, there wasn't much to say. Whilst we were sitting around drinking tea and eating Danish Pastries, Chrissy, one of the waiting staff who had been with us since the beginning, brought up the concern that she had for Jane.

"Boss, I know you have been seeing Jane. Is she alright? I heard about what happened with Peter, and I'm friends with his family. I know that they are devastated by the way he treated her."

"She's alright. She's relieved in some cases and annoyed in others, especially when she thinks about the time she wasted being with him. Tell me, Jane said that he wasn't always like that. Is it true or did she just not see the real him?"

"I've known him since we were younger, as have Jane and James. Although we were in different years, we mixed with each other a lot, and Peter was always a bit of an idiot. He was the one who would muck about in school, but then he would pull it out of the bag and become serious. Stephen and Peter used to be best friends, as well as brothers, and I know Stephen is really feeling upset over this. For no reason that anyone can work out, about a year and a half ago, Peter's attitude changed. It was like he decided he was the most important person on the earth and we all had to bow down to him. The only person's opinion that mattered was his."

"That's what Jane said, and I know she couldn't understand it either, but hopefully he has gone from her life and the damage he caused can be repaired. I liked Stephen when we met him last night. He certainly was devastated by Peter's behaviour, and I think it's going to take a long time for him to get over the betrayal and the loss of his best friend and the brother he once knew. I also know that Jane was planning on speaking to his mum and dad so that they understand that she doesn't hold anything against them."

"They would appreciate that. They love Jane and were heartbroken when they could see what he was doing to her and couldn't stop him. He just wouldn't listen to reason. Give Jane my love, won't you? You will probably see her before I do."

"Will do. Right, everyone back to work, and don't forget, if you need anything, let me know."

There were no problems at the restaurant, but I had a feeling it was going to be a weird day. Rebecca was her cheery self and as cheeky as normal. I spent a little while doing paperwork, then I went into the kitchen to chat to the chefs about the specials and to make sure they didn't need a hand. By this time, the lunch sitting was in full swing, and I chatted to some of the customers, many of whom I had met at May's barbecue. Some people would find my job tedious, but I loved it. The smiles and happiness on people's faces having good experiences in my restaurant were second to none. Just as I was laughing and chatting to Rebecca, my phone rang again. I knew it was Stephanie ringing me again. Yet again, I decided not to answer her, but my exhaustion from her constant ringing must have shown on my face because Rebecca asked me if I was ok. I wasn't going to lie to her. She knew exactly what Stephanie was like.

"For some reason, Stephanie keeps ringing me. But I'm not answering it at the moment. I don't want to speak to her."

"David, I know you're not stupid, but do you really think that is going to work? If Stephanie wants something, she knocks everyone out of the way to get it. You included."

"I answered it once and told her I wasn't interested in ever talking to her again."

"Obviously, that message hasn't sunk in. What does Jane think you should do?"

"I haven't told her about it yet because I didn't want to worry her, especially with her uncle being ill and Peter messing with her head."

"You need to tell her. Keeping it quiet will only bite you in the bum later on."

"I know, and I will. Hopefully, Stephanie will stop ringing and find some other shiny toy to play with."

"I'm not so sure she will, and I think you are being blinkered where she is concerned, and that's going to get you into trouble."

"I will be fine; I have no intention of spending any time thinking about her or dealing with her."

"On your head be it."

With that she walked away. I decided to take a break and go for a little walk along the river to try to clear my head. I knew I needed to do something about Stephanie, but I didn't want to rock the boat with Jane. Our relationship was still young, and I wanted it to last. But she was clearly still struggling with what Peter did, and I didn't want my problems to add to the burden. Walking back to the restaurant, I decided to block Stephanie's number, then she couldn't ring me. I also decided to make sure everything at the restaurant was under control and that the shut down between lunch and reopening for dinner was handled. If it was, I was going to go home and then come back later for the evening shift.

I had just got home when I received a text from Jane saying that she had just got home from work, so I thought I would ring her.

"Hello, David, I didn't expect a call."

"Afternoon, gorgeous. I have just taken a break from the restaurant before I go back in an hour for the evening shift."

"Did you want to pop round for a cup of tea if you aren't doing anything special?"

"That would be lovely, especially if you put the kettle on."

"Kettle is going on as we speak. I will see you shortly."

"You will."

It took me less than five minutes to get to Jane's house, and as promised, a cup of tea was waiting for me.

"How was your day? Did the kids behave?"

"Of course they did, especially when I told every class I had that, if they behaved, we would have a drumming competition in the last five minutes of the lesson and that the loudest class would get a treat next time we meet."

"I love that idea! I bet the other teachers love you."

"It's actually an idea we had together. All the teachers got involved and included the classes they were teaching, especially the maths class. They were collating all the votes and producing charts."

"That sounds like noisy fun whilst learning. How is the show going?"

"It's going really well; I was wondering what you were doing next week. The show is on Friday and I need help setting up everything. Normally, I'd ask James, but because he and Lacy have just got engaged and he is still trying to help my aunt, I didn't want to bother him, so I wondered if you would be able to help?"

"Of course I can! Count me in. How did your aunt take the news about Peter?"

"She was fuming, but I think James had already told her about it because the first thing she said to me was that she was proud of me."

"Told you."

"I know, and the more I think about it, the prouder I become of myself. But that's enough about me. How has today been for you?"

"It hasn't been too bad; Chrissy sends you her love, and she was telling me how bad Peter's mum and dad feel about his behaviour."

"I know. I spoke to them earlier. I'm popping round to see them later for dinner. I think it will take a while for them to believe that I don't hold them responsible for his actions."

"From what Chrissy was saying, they would really appreciate it; she seems to be worried about Stephen and how he is taking all of this."

"Honestly, so am I. I know we all had fun last night, but he looked sad, even though he was putting on a front. I'm hoping he will be there tonight so that I can offer him some support."

"You really are something special … the way you care for everyone. I have never met anyone like you before."

"I'm not that special. I just treat everyone the way I want to be treated. But I have noticed that we've shifted the conversation away from you and back onto me. So answer the question, how was your day?"

"Damn, I thought I had covered that up really well. I accomplished everything I needed to do and went through the dining room at lunchtime talking to the people that came in for lunch. Then I was starting to get a bit of a headache, so I went for a little walk along the river before I came home. I'm back at the restaurant in about half an hour to work this evening so that Rebecca can have the night off. She asked me what nights I want off, but I wanted to check with you, because if you have things planned this week, then I can work, and when you are free, I can see you then. Unless there are any emergencies, I'm off this weekend, as well."

"I'm going to see Stephen and his parents tonight, and then on Thursday I have the choir rehearsals at the community centre. At least ten people have signed up, which I was amazed about, and one night, I plan on popping over to see Auntie May. Otherwise, I'm free the rest of the week, and other than the usual household chores and marking, although I don't think there will be a lot of that this week, my weekend is clear as well."

"So, if I have Tuesday and Friday off, is that ok with you?"

"That would be great. It means I can go to my aunt's on Wednesday."

"I was wondering what you thought about going away this weekend? We could leave on Friday after work, and if you have things you need to do, we can come back early Sunday afternoon. I just thought it might do you some good to get away from it all."

"That sounds lovely! Are you ok if I leave that to you to organise?"

"Of course. I wouldn't have suggested it if I wanted you to do the arrangements. I'd better get going. I'll text you later if that's alright?"

"Of course. I think tonight is going to be hard for everyone involved."

"If you need a hug and you're passing, just pop in. I will have my arms open wide for you."

After kissing Jane goodbye, I was feeling calmer knowing that I was right about not mentioning Stephanie. Jane was balancing lots of balls, and I didn't want to add to them. I got to the restaurant just as Rebecca was putting her coat on.

"Cutting it fine, aren't you? Did you manage to sort out what nights you're working so you can give me a night or two away from your empire?"

"Don't be cheeky. Yes, is it alright if I have Tuesday and Friday off?"

"You're in charge. I'm only a mere member of staff, there for you to boss around."

"Oh, stop it. You don't change, do you?"

"Nope, and I don't intend to."

"Good. I'll see you tomorrow night. Try to have a good

night of freedom from the slave driver."

"I will."

Jane

I was a little bit nervous knocking on Peter's parents door, but as soon as Stephen opened the door, I relaxed a bit. I was shown into the living room. I was worried it would be really emotional as I had spent a lot of time here over the years and then all of a sudden I just stopped coming mainly because of the drama surrounding my breakup but also because I had been busy with my uncle's illness and school starting etc. Peter's mum, Val, was so upset. As soon as I arrived, she started crying and apologising for everything that Peter had done. It took a while to calm her down. His dad, Paul, who I always thought of as being a gentle giant, was so angry with Peter and kept asking if I was alright. Stephen made us all a cup of tea, and although he looked like he had come to terms with what had happened, like the other day in the pub, he just looked so broken.

I was worried about telling them everything he had done, but I thought it was best that they had the full story rather than having to listen to bits of gossip.

"I have missed you all that's one of the negatives of splitting up with Peter".

"I was worried you might not want to talk to us anymore and we miss you I hope that it is ok if we stay friends after all this time I see you more as a daughter and I don't really want that to change" Val said.

"I would love that although there is something I need to tell you and I would rather you heard it from me than someone else".

"Not that long after we split up I started receiving little gifts like roses and a teddy bear on my front step. There was no note so I didn't know where they came from in the end this got too much for me and James and David decided to put up one of those doorbells with cameras in them. Anyway the other day the camera showed who it was and it was Peter".

"NO" Val cried "how could he after everything he has done to you, I am so sorry".

"It's alright Val it's not your fault anyway I invited him round to my house to show him the pictures and to get him to leave me alone Connor was there but just as a witness. He wanted us to get back together but that wasn't happening. I told him that if he didn't leave me alone I would formally involve the police. He left and I thankfully I haven't seen him again".

"I thought I was ashamed about the way he treated you before but that just takes the words right out of my mouth. I am so so sorry". While Val was talking I looked over to Paul and Stephen, where Pauls face radiated anger Stephens face had gone pale and they were both having difficulty trying to come to terms with what had happened.

"No one holds any of you responsible for his behaviour. This was Peter's doing and he is the only one that should be embarrassed by his behaviour".

Apparently, Val hasn't left the house for weeks because she was worried about what people might think of her and her family.

After we talked about the hard stuff and Val had calmed down and made sure that I was ok and that no one thought ill of them, I even persuaded her to come and join the choir. It has been arranged that Paul is going to bring her along on Thursday. I did try to get him to join the choir, but apparently he is tone deaf! He even gave a sample of his singing, which was a bit painful to hear! But it eased the tension in the room somewhat, and in the end we all had a laugh at his expense, which really lightened the mood, and it was really needed.

I was tired when I got home but I really needed to see David but I didn't want to disturb him I guessed he must have been busy with the restaurant as he hadn't texted me.

David

The night was busy. Training continued with the new staff, which was going well. They were picking it up quickly. The first opportunity I got to look at the clock was when everyone had left and the restaurant was empty. It was nearly eleven o'clock. I didn't want to wake up Jane, but I had promised I would send her a message.

David: Sorry I didn't get a chance to message you earlier. Hope tonight went well. I'm here if you need me.

I wasn't expecting a reply, so was surprised when a message notification came while I was walking home.

Jane: It was hard. I've just got home if you are passing. I could really do with that cuddle.

David: Just coming now with my arms wide open.

As soon as I saw Jane open her front door, I opened my arms. She stood there, a vision of beauty, laughing at me. But despite this, getting closer, I could see the stress of the night's events on her face. She was right; she needed the cuddle. And honestly, I think I did to. I asked her how tonight went and she told me all about Peter's mum and dad and Stephen and the things that they had talked about. I am glad Peter's mum was thinking of joining the choir it will be good for her to still be part of Janes life after all her and Peter had been together for years and the bond between the parents and Jane had been established long ago.

"That sounds really good. Has anyone heard from Peter since the other night?"

"Only a text saying that he wasn't coming back. He is apparently staying with some friends in Kent and looking for a job there. Apparently, no one knew that he got sacked from work just after he moved out of mine. Not even his parents knew. Like everyone else, his workplace found his behaviour erratic, and despite being warned, he didn't do anything to improve, so eventually they got fed up and got rid of him."

"At least you don't need to worry about seeing him around town anymore, although I think a lot of the people would have chased him out of the village if they had a choice."

"I know. That's why I would never move away."

"Neither would I, now. If you are all right now and are suitably cuddled, I'd better go, but don't forget, we have a date tomorrow night. Is there anything in particular you want to do?"

"Not really. Why don't you come round here and I can cook something, as you did it last time. It won't be a patch on your cooking, but I make a really good chicken casserole using a recipe that has been passed down through generations, and even Auntie May says mine is better than hers."

"That would be lovely. I can't wait."

With that, David went home.

Chapter 8

Jane

The chicken casserole was on the hob and the bread was ready to go in the oven when David got to mine. He sent me a message when I got home from school letting me know he might be a little late as he had to stop by the kitchen. That gave me extra time to shower and put my favourite dress on. Just as I was about to check the table for about the tenth time, he arrived.

"You seem nervous. Why?" David asked just after he kissed me to say hello.

"I don't know. I think it's because I want you to enjoy your food. I've really only ever cooked for family and Peter, and surprise surprise, he wasn't impressed by my cooking. I think that's why I'm nervous."

"Well, don't be. It smells delicious, and I'm looking forward to it. I spoke to James today, and he was bigging up your casserole as well, so since then, my mouth has been watering for it."

"You know that isn't that reassuring. Now I'm worried it won't measure up to what you've been told!"

"Of course it will."

"Oh well, what's done is done. Do you want to open the wine? I just need to put the bread in the oven, which won't take long."

Dinner, as normal with David, was easy. We talked about our weekend away. Before he booked it, he thought he had better check with me as he was wondering how I felt about visiting Creswell Crags and staying nearby there. There were plenty of places to walk, and we could book some tours to go through the limestone caves and take a walk around the gorge. Although I had never been to the gorge, it sounded like something I would really enjoy, so we decided to book it.

He loved my casserole. Apparently, it was the best he'd ever had. I never realised, but when he first came to the village, he had stayed with Auntie May and had tried hers then, and apparently my casserole *was* better than hers.

Sitting in what seemed to be our usual positions on the sofa, with David in the corner and me leaning on him with his arms around my neck, fiddling with my hair, I was so relaxed I could have fallen asleep there and then.

"Do you realise how beautiful you are, not just on the outside but inside too?"

Turning around so that I could face him, I replied, "I'm not so sure about that."

"I am, and I'm also sure that you are the strongest woman I know."

I couldn't remember Peter ever calling me beautiful, let alone strong, and that was the difference between the two of them. I swallowed hard as I felt his thumb trace across my lower lip.

"Just perfect."

"Hardly." He gave me a look that was hard to describe, but the stern look in his eyes told me he wasn't joking. In the end, I muttered, "If you say so."

Sliding his hands through my hair, he held my head and looked at me. "I do," he said as his lips lowered and moved over mine in a slow, seductive way that made me feel like I was melting. Then he moved my head, angling it so that he could deepen the kiss. When his tongue slid into my mouth, I wanted to sigh.

He made me feel so safe, and I wanted to wrap my arms around his neck and return the kiss. I did so tentatively at first, but as I got used to the way that he moved, I grew more comfortable. I slid my hand beneath his shirt and ran it over his chest, feeling his hot skin. I placed my hand over his heart and felt it pounding away, smiling. I just couldn't believe I had this effect on him. And then, suddenly, my voice said,

"Should we move this to the bedroom?"

"I would love to. As long as you're sure that you're ready, because once we start, I don't think I will be able to stop, and I want you to be certain that it's what you want."

"I want *you* David." I took his hand and guided him into my bedroom. I was nervous as I had only been with one man, and look how he turned out.

I sat down on the edge of the mattress, and he kneeled in front of me. He placed his hands on my knees and slid them upwards beneath my dress, his eyes locking on me as if he needed reassurance that I was ok. He must have seen the agreement in my face as he moved fast, capturing my mouth and pushing me back on the bed. I kissed him back with everything I had, the feel of his weight on top of me just adding to the moment. Although I could feel his weight, he was holding himself up so that he didn't squash me. Moving to the left-hand side of me, his hands began to explore me while I put my hand in his hair, messing it up. I tugged hard when his large hand slid over the curve of my breast and squeezed.

My hand left his hair, gliding down his back over the tight curve of his bottom. He moved one of his legs so that it was resting between my legs. I could feel him grind up against me. I couldn't miss the hard, insistent bulge in his trousers that I had felt a few times lately when we had been kissing. I tangled my legs with his and pushed up with a whimper. I wanted more, I needed more, and I had never needed anyone as much as I needed David in that moment.

He pulled back to stand up, unbuttoning the rest of his shirt, and threw it somewhere in my bedroom. Watching me, he unbuckled his belt, slid it off, and started taking his trousers and underwear off. As soon as he was naked, he grabbed my ankles and pulled me to the edge of the and flipped me over, so that I was facing the bed. Dropping to his knees, my stomach fluttered in anticipation for what was to come. I glanced over my shoulder at him as he slid his hand under my dress and dipped his head, kissing up the back of my thighs. At the same time, his fingers hooked into my satin knickers, and he slowly pulled them down. Once they were removed, he lifted up the skirt of my dress and carried it up my body, and all I was left with was my bra. Sighing with happiness, I dropped my head against the duvet.

When he pushed my legs further apart I froze, holding my breath, waiting for his next move. He moved between my legs, and I grabbed the blanket. I wasn't sure how much more teasing I could take. Every thought I had flew out of my head as he spun me over so that I was now on my back while he continued to tease me, leaving little kisses all over my body. Not a place was missed, from the chicken pox scar to the stretch marks that were on my thighs; nothing seemed to repulse him. I had no idea where I was anymore, let alone *who* I was. All that mattered was that I was with David at last. The building pleasure of his teasing lead me to exploding, and my back arched beneath his relentless mouth with a cry. The orgasm rolled through my body, and my hips jerked with each sensation.

With a contented sigh, I looked up, and David caught me by surprise as he pulled me in towards him for a kiss whilst also undoing and taking off my bra, leaving me for the first time totally naked. There was need in his gaze, and I was over the moon to know that I was the one who had put that look on his face.

He kissed me gently then lowered his hand between our bodies and began to stroke between my thighs until I was twisting and turning beneath him, panting for him. I needed him now. The cloud in my head moved away enough for me to hear him say, "Hang on, Jane," as he left me long enough to put a condom on. As soon as that was taken care of, he lowered himself over me again and positioned himself between my legs. When our gazes met, he began to feel my body expand for him, and it was wonderful. Nothing could ever compare to this.

"Please," I begged him. He eventually took mercy on me and plunged deep inside me, and I gasped, taking him to the hilt. His hips began to rock, guiding my body with his. Slowly at first, but then faster. I felt like I was standing in the open doorway of a plane on the verge of jumping out without a parachute and only David's arms to catch me. As if he could read my mind, David whispered in my ear, "I have you. Let go." And just like that, my body exploded again. At the same time, his entire body shuddered, and a long groan escaped him as his release hit him. Lying by the side of me, David reached out and brushed a strand of hair out of my face.

"Are you ok?"

Cuddling together, I looked at him and said, "Never better." And that was how we fell asleep. I'm not sure either of us planned to end up in that position, but that was how I woke up the next morning, looking at him smiling at me still in his arms.

"Morning," he said as he kissed my nose. "Are you ok? I didn't mean to stay the night without asking, but I guess we were both tired."

"I would have been upset if you hadn't. I'm glad you're here." I groaned. "I don't really want to leave the bed, but I need to get breakfast and get ready for school."

"Why don't you get ready for school and I will make you breakfast? Do you have the ingredients to make pancakes?"

"Yes! I love pancakes but never get round to making them."

"Alright then, pancakes and coffee on order."

Getting out of bed was hard. For the first time in a long time, I felt relaxed, loved, and cherished. No wonder Lacy walked round permanently happy all the time. I knew it was too early to say the 'love' word, but that was how I felt, although I decided to keep that to myself for the time being. I didn't want to jump in too quickly, but I felt a lot closer to David than I ever did with Peter. Whilst Peter and I grew up together, I knew more about David's likes and true personality than I ever did Peter's.

The pancakes that David made were ready for me as soon as I'd had my shower and got dressed, and they were wonderful. He had even made a berry compote to go with them! Because he had made breakfast, it meant that I had a little more time than I normally did before I had to leave. Instead of running out of the door, hoping that I hadn't forgotten anything, I had my bags packed with lesson plans, packed lunch, which David had also made, and everything I needed for that day and for the visit to see my aunt and uncle straight after work. Leaving the house and kissing David goodbye before we went in our different directions, him to his house to get changed and mine to work for the day, I could see that it going to be a good day and nothing could change that.

Nothing did. Not even the teasing I got from Sam when I was at work and the cross-examination she tried to give me or the ribbing I got from James when I saw him at my aunt's house.

I was sure he had come by just to wind me up, but it didn't work. David and I had exchanged a few texts during the day and evening and a phone call as soon as he finished work when I was in bed. Thursday was just the same as I got a text as soon as I was up, wishing me a good day. Then another one later on in the day, wishing me good luck with the choir practice, and another phone call at night-time, reassuring me that everything was booked for the weekend and that he couldn't wait to see me Friday night.

David

On Friday, I got to Jane's house at five o'clock. She was already packed and ready to go, so after she locked the house up, we set off. I had booked us into a cottage near Mansfield, which was approximately an hour and a half away from Greengrove, which meant that we got there just before seven o'clock. The keys had been left in a locked box by the front door. On opening the doorway, we walked into a lovely hallway, which had some original bricks exposed on the top half while the bottom half of the wall was plastered with white paint. The lovely tranquil feel continued throughout the cottage, with all the rooms a lovely clean magnolia colour with various photos hanging on the walls in each room. The living room had a comfortable, velvet, dark blue sofa, a TV, some bookshelves with guidebooks, a fire, a round dining table, and four chairs. The bathroom had a walk-in shower and a gift box with everything one might need for a few nights away. Although the kitchen was small, it was functional, with a built-in oven and microwave. I had brought some food from my restaurant for our dinner. It was a fairly simple dinner of cheese and bread, with chocolate cake for pudding, but I decided there was nothing better than a Friday evening sitting in front of the fire with a glass of wine and some cheese and bread, watching the TV, cuddled up on the sofa. We went to bed early because I had planned a full day at Creswell Crags.

After warming up some croissants, we left the cottage and went to the Creswell Crags for the day. The sun was shining, and we couldn't have asked for a better day. I packed a picnic, which we left it in the car while we went on the cave tour, but first, we walked around the grounds. The limestone gorge was breath-taking. We walked past the children's play area, with climbing frames in the shape of dinosaurs, and following the path, we came across some striking limescale cliffs with a river running between them. People were walking on either side of the river. We decided to walk past the river, heading further into the woodland, as according to the map that we had picked up from the information desk, we would be walking along one of the sides of river when we went on our cave tour. We walked for about forty-five minutes before we decided it was time to follow the path back so that we could have our picnic lunch before our cave tour started at 2 o'clock. Sitting on one of the picnic benches with our small picnic of sandwiches, quiche, and crisps, it was lovely and peaceful, although there were people around. The noise they made seemed to evaporate, plus you couldn't hear the sound of any nearby roads. Soon, it was time for us to take part in the tour. We joined eight other people for the tour, and after the safety briefing, we put on our hard hats with torches on the top and set off walking back towards the water and turned right, walking past the cliffs towards the cave where we were going to investigate. Inside the cave, the tour guide told us about the cave and how it was used. He was really knowledgeable, explaining the history of the caves and demonstrating some of the tools that were used. Even the most obscure questions he managed to answer.

Although donning a hard hat is not most people's idea of a perfect date, to me it was great, and I knew Jane felt the same way because the smile on her face and the enthusiasm she had when we visited the museum, which was also on site. In the end, we spent the whole day there, only leaving when the museum closed. On the way back to the cottage, we stopped off at a lovely pub, which had been recommended to us by the hosts of the cottage. I had wanted to take Jane somewhere quiet, cosy, and with great food. Although the weekend was only short, it was a little escapism, which we both needed to recharge our batteries.

Sitting in the pub, sharing a mixed meat platter, Jane said,

"I really appreciate you organising this weekend. It has been so relaxing. I don't think I have ever had such a wonderful, relaxed time away."

"It was my pleasure, I'm glad you enjoyed it. You certainly deserve it. It's just a pity we couldn't manage a few more days. Maybe when school breaks up, we can come back and visit more of the caves."

"I would love that. Everything has been perfect. Did you say we had to leave before ten tomorrow morning?"

"Yes, check out is at ten. Was there anything you wanted to do before we went home?"

"Would you mind if we stopped at my aunt and uncle's for lunch? I would like to see them, if that's alright?"

"Of course that's fine. Do you want to ring her to let her know?"

"Great, I can just text her. She offered the other day but I forgot to mention it till now."

"That's a plan, then. We should be at their house around noon."

"Thanks, I will text her now."

After our wonderful platters, it didn't take long to get

back to the cottage, where we sat in front of the fire resting after our busy day. I was starting to fall asleep when I realised that Jane had actually fallen asleep. Waking her up, we went to bed, where I had a lovely comfortable sleep.

Packing up didn't take long in the morning, and we were on our way home by nine thirty. May had a lovely roast beef meal waiting for us. By the time we'd had lunch and had stayed a while talking to May, Mike, James, and Lacy, we didn't get back to Jane's house until eight o'clock, and I decided to only come inside for a quick visit. We didn't set the village alight that night while we said goodnight before separating to get ready for another week.

It was the week of her school concert, so I knew she would be busy, and I had promised that I would be there to help get everything ready. We got to the hall early on Friday afternoon. I managed to get Rebecca to cover me in the restaurant for the evening shift so that I could be here and help Jane throughout the night. It was amazing seeing her working. The smile on her face was one of complete joy. Nothing seemed to phase her, and I could tell she was happy being a teacher. She knew all the kids really well; which ones were going to have stage fright, which ones were going to play up. One thing was for certain; when stressed, she didn't let the kids know. She was taking charge of the backstage set up while I was putting out the chairs, helping to get the programmes together, so I didn't see much of her, but whenever I did, that smile was there. The kids had arrived but it wasn't long before one of them came and asked me, "Are you Miss's boyfriend? My mum said you were." Just as I was about to answer, Jane came out of nowhere and said, "Yes, he is. Now, this isn't where you are supposed to be, is it, Joseph?"

"No miss. My mum said he's so much better looking than Peter and a lot nicer." With a shy smile, Joseph ran off.

"His mum is right. You *are* better looking and a lot nicer than Peter." With that, she walked away, turning back briefly to smile at me.

I was speechless at that declaration, laughing at myself. I returned to clearing the stage. That was the last I saw of Jane until the end of the concert, which was amazing, with many of the children enjoying themselves and showing their parents what they could do. A lot of proud people left the hall, and although Jane was exhausted, she was overwhelmed with parents coming up to her and thanking her for instilling confidence and enjoyment in their children. We spent the weekend together, not really doing much, and then went to her aunt's for the weekly barbeque, where I did my share of the cooking. Now that Mike was on the mend, he wanted to try to do some cooking. Apparently, he looked forward to it, so with us both at the helm and Jane, Lacy, and May doing the vegetables and salad, we left James in charge of the drinks.

During the next four weeks, we slipped into a pattern. On Thursdays, Jane had choir practice, and I had two nights off each week. Because of the extra staff I had employed, it meant I could have most weekends off as Rebecca would cover the weekends. We spent a lot of time between both mine and Jane's houses. At the weekend, we were at her house, and during the week we stayed at mine. I was under no illusions: I knew I loved her, but I was still a bit wary of telling her. Not just because of the trouble she had gone through with Peter, but also because of the damage my ex-wife had caused to me mentally, and although I knew Jane wouldn't throw my love back at me, I was still cautious. It had been a few weeks since I had last heard from Stephanie. For that I was relieved, also because I hadn't told Jane that she had got in contact. I was sure she had moved onto another victim.

Life was easy. We were at my house just getting ready to go to Auntie May's barbeque when my doorbell rang. I was in the middle of putting the ribs I had marinated overnight into a bag to take them with me, so Jane answered the door.

"Who are you? What are you doing in my husband's house?"

"Who are you?" Jane's voice sounded strained.

"Damn," I said to myself. Rebecca was right. Not mentioning Stephanie was going to bite me in the bum, and I could feel it now. Quickly washing my hands, I went to the door.

"I am your *ex*-husband, Stephanie. What do you want?"

"Don't be like that, darling. I told you on the phone that it was a little mistake and didn't mean anything. You and I are meant to be together. You know that. You read my texts."

"No. No way. I am finally happy. Just go away and leave me alone. Hang on, how do you know where I live?"

"I asked someone at the village shop. They seem to know everything. When we move back to London, you will be able to sneeze without everyone bringing you soup."

I didn't know what to say. I just stood there, dumbfounded on the doorstep with Jane and Stephanie. Eventually, Jane spoke.

"Oh yes, in fact, as soon as we see someone get a handkerchief out, we tell everyone to get the broth going. You have to catch it quick, you know."

"Charming. David, I don't know who she is, but you need to get rid of her so that we can talk." And with that, Stephanie pushed herself past Jane and marched into the living room.

Taking a deep breath, I finally looked at Jane, who looked confused.

"That is my ex-wife. Is it alright if you go to the barbeque without me? I will come as soon as I can. I need to sort this out."

"Are you sure? I can wait."

"No, it's ok. If you take the ribs, I won't be far behind you."

Just as I was about to lean over and kiss her, Stephanie put her head round the door and said, "Oh, you're still here. Why haven't you left yet?"

"Oh, don't worry, I'm just leaving," replied Jane. "I would say it's nice meeting you, but I was brought up not to lie. So goodbye. I hope I never see you again." And just like that, Jane left. I really hoped she knew how much she meant to me and that she wasn't annoyed with me for keeping secrets from her, but I needed to get rid of Stephanie now then make sure Jane was alright. Taking a deep breath, I turned to talk to Stephanie.

"What are you doing here?"

"I want you, David. I've always wanted you. I made a mistake, but there has been no one else like you in my life. We need to try again."

"It was a hell of a mistake. You were having an affair before we even got married! If you hadn't been so careless about who you sent that text to, I may never have found out. As far as I'm concerned, I made the mistake of believing anything you said. I am not stupid, and I have no desire to make that mistake again. Besides, I no longer love you. That isn't even the most important reason why we're not getting back together. I love the wonderful woman you were just incredibly rude to. She is the most genuine, loveable, strong woman I have ever met, and for everything you are, she is a hundred times better."

"How dare you speak to me like that?"

"Well, they do say the truth hurts. Now, you need to leave because I have a wonderful woman waiting for me at a lovely, friendly, community barbeque, which you would hate. Oh, and by the way, Jane is James' cousin. You remember James? He doesn't like you much."

She scoffed. "What am I going to do now, David?"

"You are going to leave this house and this village. After that, I have no idea, and I don't really care."

I stood there, holding the door open as Stephanie flounced out, and I closed it before she could say anything else.

I thought I had better text Rebecca to let her know that her sister was around and that she was right: ignoring Stephanie had come back at me. After a little while, once I had calmed down, I went off to the barbeque to make sure Jane was ok.

Jane

Meeting David's ex-wife was interesting. She was nothing like I thought she would be. I imagined she would look like one of those high maintenance people you see around; you know, the ones with perfect make up, not a hair out of place, size eight, with not one curve, and fake nails. She was all that and more. She walked as if she owned the world, like we were all below her. Her clothes fitted perfectly, and there wasn't a crease on anything she wore. I had never asked David what she did for a living, but I bet she wasn't a teacher. The strange thing was, I didn't feel threatened by her. In fact, between us, I more of a catch, and she should be frightened by me. The more I thought about Stephanie doing a hard day's work, the funnier it got. Walking out to the back garden at my aunt's, I laughed to myself.

"Someone looks happy. What's so funny?" James walked up to me, taking the ribs off me and kissing my cheek.

"Stephanie, David's ex-wife," I replied.

"I'm not sure I could say that about her. Why is she funny?"

"I was thinking about what she might do for a living because I don't think it was ever mentioned, and then I started going through careers options. I mean, the idea of her with her perfect nails as a bin lorry driver … you have to admit, it's quite funny."

"That woman wouldn't know what hard work is. Where is David?"

"She is the reason why David isn't here yet. I opened his

door and was confronted by her asking for her husband."

"Is David ok? Do you think I should go help him get rid of the rubbish?"

"I think he will be just fine, although he may need rescuing when I give him a piece of my mind about keeping secrets. Apparently, she had been messaging and ringing him."

"You're not worried about her, are you?"

"Not at all. I haven't a doubt that he wants rid of her, especially when I saw his face when she was rude to me and when she was rude about the village."

"Good. He loves you, Jane. She did a number on him when he found out that she had been having an affair. But he's happy here, and when I have asked in the past if he would move back to London, he asked me if I was mad. Come on, let's put these on the barbeque."

The next thing I heard was David shout, "Move away from my ribs, James. You are not to touch them!" Turning round, I saw that David had just come into the back garden through the side gate.

"Who knew me getting near food would upset you so much? I hear you had to put the rubbish out before you could come."

"I did," David replied, pulling me towards him and putting his arm around me. He asked me if I was ok.

"There is nothing wrong with Jane. She was laughing earlier about your ex-wife being a bin lorry driver. Honestly, once she put that image in my head, I couldn't get it out. I mean, can you imagine her perfect nails and extensions by the time she finished her shift?" James replied for me.

"I would pay good money to see that!" David laughed before turning to me. James gave us a moment alone. "You didn't think that I would want her over you, do you?"

"Not for a minute, although we do need to have a chat about keeping secrets."

"I know. I'm sorry. Rebecca said I should have told you, but I just didn't know how to, especially as the first time she contacted me was while we were dealing with Peter."

"How did Rebecca know?"

"I told her. Stephanie is Rebecca's older sister. They have been estranged ever since we split up. In fact, she hasn't spoken to her since then."

"Wow, I never knew that. Although that is yet another secret you have kept from me. Does she know that she visited?"

"I know. I'm sorry. Yes, I messaged her on my way over

here. She doesn't think she will visit the restaurant, but she is ready if she does. Stephanie thrives on the power of catching you unawares."

"I can't believe they are sisters. They're total opposites."

"I know. I'd better go and put the ribs on before James decides to touch them."

"Ok, I'm going to help Lacy and my aunt make the sides."

The barbeque was a wild affair. Well, as wild as Greengrove events normally are. The men were trying to outdo each other, playing football or running races with the children in the field. The women sat on the other side of the field, laughing at the men. I was sitting there, laughing at the antics that James and David were getting up to. They were trying to play football on the field opposite May's house with some of the other men, but because they were on opposing teams, they spent more time holding onto each other so they couldn't get the ball than actually playing.

"I don't understand those two. Everything has to be a competition. If they really thought about it and actually played on the same team, they would win with no problem, but no. They are too busy trying to be the best." Lacy laughed as she sat down.

"I know. Men! They're really just big kids. We should get some kind of medal for putting up with them."

Just as I was saying that, Auntie May walked over to where we were sitting in the garden, watching the two of them. "How do you think I feel? I had the pair of them living with me for a while. At least you two can share the burden between you."

"That's true! Where is Uncle Mike? I can't see him."

"He went to sit in the living room with a group of his old cronies, putting the world to rights."

"Back to his old self, then."

"Yep, but enough about us! How are you? I heard you met the wonderful Stephanie and lived to tell the tale."

"I did. She really is something. Have you ever met her, Lacy?"

"No, I haven't," Lacy replied, "and I'm guessing from what you're saying, I don't want to, either."

"You really don't. You know, thinking about it, she and Sarah might be from the same mould. In fact, if they didn't live in different parts of the country, I would think they were the same person."

"I had hoped there was only one Sarah. Which reminds me - did someone tell you that she has decided to move away? She got a transfer at work to London and has terminated her lease, so she can go now."

"Now *that* is good news. Although I pity London because now they have her *and* David's ex-wife. I hope London is ready for them."

"I doubt anyone or anything is ready for the two of them." Just as we were finishing our drinks, James and David came up, and just as James was about to open his mouth, David beat him to the punch.

"How are the three most beautiful women getting on?"

"Damn, David, I was going to say that!" James grumbled, and the three of us burst out laughing, with David and James looking confused. Standing up, May kissed them both on the cheek and said, "Don't worry, we're only laughing at you." She left leaving Lacy and me in stitches.

The barbeque was starting to wind down as people got together to put their chairs away. After giving our partners a kiss each, Lacy and I went inside to help tidy up while the boys reorganised the outside space.

"Jane, I wanted to ask …" Lacy began. "I know a while ago we talked about you restarting your business of singing at events, and I know how busy things have been with the Peter drama, Uncle Mike's illness, the restart of the choir, and the school concert … but I wondered if you had thought any more about the events?"

"I totally forgot about it! But in my heart, I'm not sure that I can commit to restarting it, with school and spending time with David and everything else. I don't know where I would put the hours in. Why?"

"I have a bride that had a wedding singer all booked, but, despite paying the deposit, the singer has disappeared and isn't responding to messages. She is reluctant to find another one in case the same thing happens again, and they don't have much spare money as they are paying for it all by themselves."

"When is the wedding?"

"Well, that's the other problem. It's next Saturday. She only wanted someone to sing for the first dance and a few other songs before they have a DJ later on."

I smiled at her. "I owe you a favour. Unless David has arranged anything for us next weekend, I will do it free of charge, as long as I know what I am singing by Wednesday at the latest. But let me check with David first."

"Check what with me?" David said as he and James entered the kitchen. Lacy and I explained. "I haven't made any plans," David said. "And if I had, we could cancel them. I think you should do it. You love singing, and I know we have talked a little bit about why you can't commit to restarting your business, but a few events here or there is giving you the best of both worlds, especially if I come along as your roadie, then I get to hear your wonderful voice as well."

It really made a difference having a partner who supported me and wanted to share everything with me. Before I could think of any more excuses, I told Lacy I would do it.

After saying goodbye to everyone, it didn't take long to get to David's house. I needed to say my piece about him keeping secrets from me, and I decided I would rather do it now instead of letting it fester.

"David, we need to talk."

"We do. I'm sorry."

"I know you are, but I love you, David, and I don't want to go back to having a relationship that isn't equal, and that is what happens if there are secrets. I can understand a little bit why you didn't tell me when she first called you, but you had plenty of time afterwards. I think you should tell me everything now, don't you?"

I didn't mean to tell him I loved him, it just slipped out. But to be honest, I was relieved that I'd said it, I had been worried about declaring my love for him, worrying if I was reading too much into our relationship. But I knew that I needed to let go of those three words that meant so much to me.

"You're right. I love you too, more than anything, and certainly more than I ever loved *her*. I think I was frightened that she would ruin everything for me. She called me a couple of months ago and asked if she could see me, but I said no, I didn't want to see her. She then called a few more times, but I never answered. I also received a few texts, but after a week of that, I decided to block her number, and obviously I never heard from her again. And because of that, I honestly forgot about it, and as time went on, it was a case of out of sight out of mind.. But I was stupid to think that, and Rebecca warned me not to underestimate her and to tell you, but with all the things that were happening at that time, I didn't want to upset you anymore. I really am sorry, and if I could turn the clock around and re-do things, I would. Please believe me. Like I said, it was stupid of me."

"I don't think you were stupid. Blinkered, yes, but not stupid. There are no other secrets you're keeping from me?"

"No, that was it, and from now on, I am following the saying 'a problem shared is a problem halved', and our ex-partners seem to be problems we have both had."

"We really did pick badly the first time. Thankfully, our luck is improving."

"It is. I love you, Jane, and I know that this might seem quick and a bit rash, but you are it for me, Jane, and now that our exes have stopped causing chaos in our lives, I feel that the time is right, so I was wondering if you would do the honour of marrying me? I know it might be a bit early, but I am not going to change my mind."

"David!" I tried to get his attention, but he carried on speaking.

"I knew I would fall for you when I heard that wonderful voice of yours in the pub. If you want a long engagement, we can do that, but I would rather we get married next year. But it is up to you. That is if you say yes. I don't want to put pressure on you to say yes, just because I asked you now. I want you to know that you can say no, but as long as we are together, I am willing to wait until you are ready."

"Have you finished? You didn't let me get a word in edgeways." David pretended to zip his mouth shut and gave me an imploring look. "Yes, I would like to marry you. No, I don't think it's too soon as the things we have gone through already make me certain that it is the right thing to do, and, yes, next year would be a perfect time to get married."

"You would? You do?"

"Yes. Now let's celebrate in the bedroom." I gave him a cheeky grin.

And that was what we did. We didn't resurface till

the next morning. As usual, David got the breakfast ready while I showered. When I went to sit down at the table to my pancakes, this time with syrup, sitting there in the middle of the pancake on a upside down egg cup was an open ring box with the most beautiful ruby red and diamond ring. The ruby was square with diamonds surrounding it, and the gold band was twisted and open cut. It really was the most beautiful thing I had ever seen.

"I don't know what to say."

"I didn't want to put the ring box directly on the pancake in case it ruined the pancake, and I knew you would never forgive me if that happened. So, I improvised."

"You certainly did. The ring looks amazing. I have never seen anything so beautiful before."

"I doubt that. Don't you look in the mirror every morning?"

"That is too cheesy for this time of the morning," I said, laughing at him. He lifted the box off the egg cup and took the ring out, placing it on my engagement finger. With tears running down my face, I kissed him before panic hit me. "Oh, quick, I need to phone Auntie May to tell her. If she hears it from anyone else, she will never forgive me."

"Calm down, she has probably already heard about our engagement, because I asked your uncle last night if I could marry you. He looked totally taken aback, and then he said he would be honoured to give his permission. He has probably already told your aunt to expect a call."

"It means so much to me that you asked my uncle. I really do love you. I need to phone my auntie, but first I am eating this delicious-looking pancake, although if you keep feeding me like this, I'm going to need to go on a diet just to fit down any aisle."

"No, you don't. You are perfect just the way you are and always will be. Now eat."

I phoned Auntie May, and, before I could even get a word in, she said, "Well?"

As soon as I told her that I said yes and that we wanted to get married next year, she was over the moon, especially as James and Lacy had just told her that they had booked their wedding for the 10th May next year. Auntie May and Uncle Mike had already decided to have a family dinner at James' pub so that we could share the good news and show off my ring. Uncle Mike had told her it was the most beautiful ring he had ever seen, obviously except for the one he had bought my aunt. After a little while, we ended the conversation and agreed that we would meet in the pub that night.

Sitting round the table with my family meant so much

to me. I suggested David invited Rebecca as she was his family, which he did, and she came. It did mean that the restaurant was managerless for the night, but apparently Chrissy who had worked at the restaurant since it opened had volunteered to step into the position. Auntie May launched into Rebecca as soon as she arrived and welcomed her to the family. I could tell that she was a bit taken aback. When everyone was ordering drinks, Lacy and I tag teamed her. Each of us holding her hand, we both said at the same time, "Don't worry, you get used to it. But now you won't ever get away. May has decided you are part of the family."

With tears in her eyes, she said, "I don't know what to say. I wasn't expecting this, and to be accepted for who I am, after everything my sister did, is just overwhelming."

"I know, but as we told Peter's family, you cannot be held accountable for other people's actions. Now dry those tears, David is looking concerned. I will introduce you to all your extended family; in other words, the whole village."

David

James and I went to get the drinks in whilst everyone chatted. Looking over at my fiancée, whilst she was talking to an overwhelmed Rebecca, I couldn't stop smiling.

"Stop looking like you want to eat her. That's my cousin, you know."

"I know, and despite that, I still love her."

"Congratulations, you have woken up and realised that the grass is definitely greener on this side of the fence."

"Who knew all those years ago when we met at university that we would end up being related?"

"Not me! But I'm glad we will be. Come on, let's take the drinks to the table and let our eyes glaze over as the women we love talk about weddings."

"I can't think of anywhere I would rather be."

"Actually, neither can I."

With smiles on our faces, we carried the drinks back to the table for what seemed to be a little impromptu gathering of people wishing us congratulations. I had a few people tell me that if I upset Jane, I would have them to answer to. I told them I had no desire to upset her; in fact, I never wanted to see her upset ever again, and I would walk over hot coals to make sure that didn't happen. After we put the glasses down and everyone was seated, I proposed a toast to New Beginnings. With that, we all chinked our glasses together and said, "New Beginnings!"

James, Mike, and I started talking about the latest sports news and what was happening in the hospitality sector and the changes that were being made to the licencing and labelling of food, whilst Jane, Lacy, Rebecca, and May were talking amongst themselves. It was only as we left that night that I realised the wedding planning had already started and was in full force. I had never known an engagement meal turn into a total wedding planning session before, although to be honest this was my first engagement meal. When I'd got engaged with Stephanie, she had gone out with her friends and left me at home on my own. But by the time we had left the pub, Jane had asked both Rebecca and Lacy to be bridesmaids. It was decided that the wedding would be in the private room of the restaurant, which we would completely closed for the day. Luckily I had previously already decided because of the restaurants location to apply for a licence to hold civil marriages on the premises and that had just come through, because Lacy had her own wedding to organise, her business partner at Especially Yours would be in charge of our wedding. Never did I think I would be getting married again, but there I was, the luckiest person around, and I was loving every minute of it.

Epilogue

One year Later.

May and Mike's house.

Jane

Standing in front of the full-length mirror in my room at my aunt and uncle's house, I couldn't believe my eyes. Looking back at me, wearing a white mermaid-style dress with a sweetheart neckline, was a woman who looked so happy and carefree, without a worry in the world, and that was exactly how I felt. I couldn't believe this day had finally arrived, and nothing could put a dampener on it. Auntie May was helping me get ready. I wished my mum was there, but I wouldn't ask for anyone else to help me get ready.

"You look so beautiful; your mum would have been so proud of you." Auntie May looked up at me with tears in her eyes.

"Thank you, Auntie. I miss her so much. But knowing that you're here with me means so much to me. I just hope this mascara is as waterproof as it says it is, otherwise I'll be walking down the aisle with ruined make up."

"I don't think David would mind how you walk down

that aisle, as long as you walk towards him."

"That's true."

"Knock knock."

"Come in, Uncle Mike."

"Has my wife made you cry yet or did she break first?"

"She broke first, but it was a close-run thing."

"We are so proud of you, and David is a wonderful man. You picked a good one."

"Thank you, Uncle."

"Right, May, out you go, and send Lacy in here. It's time to get this show on the road. We will see you at the wedding."

"Love you both." She kissed both Mike and I and left to get into Lily's car to take her to the wedding.

"I am honoured that you asked me to walk you down the aisle today."

"I can't think of anyone else I would rather have with me. You have been like a dad to me for so long that I'm sure I sometimes forget you are my uncle."

"That's fine by me. You're more my daughter than my niece. Now let's get going and marry you off so that I can have a son-in-law to go with my wonderful daughter-in-law."

Just as he said that, Lacy entered the room to tell us that the car was here. Uncle Mike and I just burst out laughing. The timing was perfect. But our laughter left Lacy looking confused, which made us laugh more.

Fish On the River

David

Standing in the function room in my suit, I gazed at the way we had reorganised the chairs into six on each side with an aisle in the middle. The chairs were starting to fill up. People walked past me with a mixture of greetings from "Good luck", to "Congratulations", and "You're a lucky man." I couldn't believe this day was finally here. I may have been married before but being with Jane wasn't like my previous marriage. She was my partner, my best friend, and the love of my life, who made me laugh and actually cared about me. Just as I was standing there, stuck in my own head, James walked up.

"I don't think I have ever seen you as nervous as you are now," he said as he patted me on the back. He was right. I had never been this nervous, and I wasn't sure why I was now. I did know that I didn't want anything to go wrong today. Jane deserved the world, and I aimed to give it to her.

"Before I forget, thank you for being my best man. I couldn't think of anyone better than my best friend. And I know you and Jane are like brother and sister. I appreciate it."

"Stop it, you will make me blush. Now straighten your tie. The woman of the moment has arrived."

"About time." I could hear the violins playing Canon in D from the speakers, and I turned round and there she was. The most beautiful bride I had ever seen, and she was walking towards me. Seeing my future wife walking towards me was the most beautiful sight I had ever seen. She was glowing from head to toe, and I knew then that I was the happiest man alive. I wanted to give Jane the wedding of her dreams. Although I had been married before, this was going to be her first and only wedding, and she deserved it. I still had money from my house sale, which we had used for the wedding, but I would have paid double that to see her smile.

The ceremony went through in a flash, and before you knew it, we were downstairs in the restaurant having our wedding meal. Every now and then, I couldn't help but look over at Jane and smile. Just as the empty plates were taken away, Mike stood up to start the speeches.

"I would like to thank you all for coming to witness the joining of these two wonderful people. I was honoured to be asked by Jane to be her father figure on this wonderful occasion. I have always loved and cherished Jane as I would any daughter we could have had. I will never forget the day I met Jane as I helped her mum leave the hospital. As the official driver, I took this wonderful bundle of joy and put her in her car seat, and just as I was securing her in, she looked up and smiled at me with her dimples on show. From that moment on, I knew there would be two women in my life who I would do anything for; my wonderful wife and Jane. I thought about telling a funny story about Jane, but I know it would embarrass her too much, and I don't want to get on the wrong side of her, because she can make the best banana and chocolate chip cake I have ever tasted! I do want to say that both her aunt and I, and I know her mum as well, are all proud of her. She has shown that with determination and pure stubbornness, she can achieve what she wants. So, watch out David." The whole room rang with laughter.

"Could I ask that you all please stand with me and raise your glass to toast David and Jane as I hand her over to David. I know he will love and cherish her every bit as much as my wife and I do. To the happy couple. May your love and future be as strong as mine and May's."

I wasn't sure how I could top that speech, but as I stood up to reciprocate, all the nerves left me as I took Jane's hand in mine.

"Thank you, Mike and May. My wife and I would like to thank everyone for coming, especially those who have helped us in the run up for today; Mike and May for their never-ending support; James and Lacy, the most wonderful best man and bridesmaid a couple could ever have; Lorraine, one of the best wedding planners around; and all the staff at the restaurant, especially Rebecca, who not only was a bridesmaid but also helped get the restaurant looking as beautiful as it is. Although, I have just noticed she has left her seat, probably to interfere somewhere: she did, after all, learn from the best! And last but not least, I want to thank my wonderful wife. You have made me the happiest I have ever been. I am so grateful that I managed to get the night off work to hear you sing at James and Lacy's engagement party. When I looked over and saw you that night, I had no idea what hit me. I would like everyone to raise their glasses and toast to family, friends, and those who couldn't be here with us today. You are with us in spirit. Without further ado, I would like to pass you over to my best man, who, I hope after his speech, will still be my best friend. James."

"Thank you. All of you here know how special these two are, although David isn't as good as me, because I am, after all, the *best* man. Jane bought me some socks that say that in case I forgot my role today. Well, that's what *she* said. I thought it was because she was just reaffirming something I have been telling her for years. Anyway, I digress. These two people are very special to me. Obviously, I have known Jane all my life. Although she is my cousin, I see her more as my sister, and, like my dad, I could tell you a few stories to embarrass her, but I also value my life, and thankfully, brides don't tend to have best men at weddings. When I researched what I should include for my speech, nothing said 'embarrass the bride'. It did, however, say you are allowed to embarrass the groom with a funny story, so here goes. When I first met David, we were just walking into our second week of university and studying a Customer Service module. We went into the lecture hall and sat side by side. After we introduced ourselves to each other, in walked the visiting lecturer. Unbeknownst to the rest of the class, David had had an interview with him for a job in his restaurant while he was studying, and, as I found out later, it didn't turn out that well. Apparently, he wasn't a pleasant man towards his staff or customers, and although David got the job, he decided he didn't want it and found a waiting job in another restaurant. Anyway, picture the scene: the man at the front is talking about how the customer is right and how if there are any problems then they should be treated calmly and with no embarrassment towards the staff or customers. Every now and then, I could hear David mutter under his breath. He started asking questions based on the experience he'd had. Things like, what do you believe managers should do if staff are being shouted at by customers? Should all members of staff feel that the manager supports them and how? I could go on. Anyway, after five minutes of these questions, the man gave up, and as his face was getting redder and redder, I was concerned that he was going to have a heart attack. In the end, he told us all to leave. I asked David what his issue was with the bloke, and when he told me, I agreed with his reasoning, but, as I told him at the time, it would have been better if David hadn't been sitting there with his flies undone! Now that I have made you all laugh, and also check your trousers, I want to honestly say, welcome to the family, David. I have always thought of you as my brother, and I am very happy that it was you who married Jane. I couldn't think of anyone better. Please raise your glasses to the happy couple."

The rest of the night went quickly, and other than when we cut the cake and had our first dance, I didn't spend much time with my bride, so I was glad when the car arrived to take us to the hotel we were staying at before we started our honeymoon the next day in Paris. I finally spotted her talking to May. Walking over to her and touching her back, I smiled at her. "Are you ready, my darling wife? The car is here to whisk us away."

"I am, my husband," she said, turning to her aunt. "Thank you again for everything you did for us. But if you will excuse us, my husband says my chariot awaits."

"Don't be silly. Stop saying thank you. I love you like you're mine. Of course I will do anything for you. Now, off you go you two, and enjoy yourselves. We will see you in two weeks." She gave us both a kiss and cuddle and sent us away.

Sitting in the car, I said to my wife, "I love you," and she replied, "I love you too."

With that, we started our married life, and I was looking forward to spending my forever with Jane.

Creswell Crags

Crags Road, Welbeck, Worksop,

Nottinghamshire, S80 3LH

creswell-crags.org.uk

In this book, David and Jane visit Creswell Crags as part of a weekend away. I decided, after visiting this wonderful place, that it was an excellent place to visit if you wanted to get away from all the stresses of life. Below is some information on the Crags, and I hope it inspires you to visit this wonderful place as well.

Creswell Crags in North Nottinghamshire is a limestone gorge, honeycombed with caves and smaller fissures. Stone tools and remains of animals found in the caves by archaeologists provide evidence for a fascinating story of life during the last Ice Age between 50,000 and 10,000 years ago. Further evidence came to light in 2003 with the discovery of Britain's only known Ice Age rock art. It is also home to the biggest concentration of 'witches' marks' found in British caves. 'Apotropaic' marks were scribed into the cave surface as they were thought to keep evil spirits coming from the underworld. Hundreds of these protective marks, believed to be from the 17th and 18th centuries, were discovered in 2018.

By booking the various guided tours, you can visit some of the caves and listen to the wonderful guides pass on information on the specific caves and answer any questions you may have.

About the Author

Helen is a mother of two grown up daughters living in North Yorkshire. History and research have always been something she has loved, and she has three master's degrees in History, which she did later in life. She has always wanted to write, but due to being diagnosed as dyslexic later in life, she always thought it was something she couldn't do, but she is proving herself wrong. Helen loves reading and visiting different places in the United Kingdom, especially if they have canals or waterfalls. This is where the inspiration for Greengrove comes from.

Helen can be found on these social media pages:
Facebook: Helen Kelly Books
Twitter: @happy_eeyore
helenkellyauthor.com

Hold Me

Greengrove Book 3

Debbie

Over the last few years, I have struggled with my health. I was embarrassed to leave the house until my twin sister, Dawn, persuaded me that I should do something away from my house as I work from home. In the end, I gave in and joined the community centre choir, which our friend Jane had set up. Little did I realise that joining the choir would change my life so much.

Connor

I have lived in Greengrove all my life, and after being promoted to sergeant of the local police force, I was lucky enough to be able to continue working in the local police station. During my time off, I take part in triathlons. One of the things about living and working in Greengrove is that you know everyone, and as a result, trying to find my special person has been difficult - until I saw Debbie in a different way.